"Linnet, we could still make it good, we *have* to."

"All it takes," Piers continued, "is a little forgiveness on both sides."

"I don't want your forgiveness," she sneered. "I want you to turn the page."

"Isn't that what I've been suggesting?" His deep soft voice was almost hypnotic. "What we had, we still have." His arms slid around her and drew her close.

It was happening again, as she'd known it would. She was pressing herself against him almost crying with pleasure until she heard what he was murmuring against the softness of her throat. "This time there'll be no more Archies...." It wasn't love he was offering, only lust—maybe he was even saving face.

"No!" It came out as a hoarse dry mutter. "I don't want to spend the rest of my life making the best of a bad job...."

JENETH MURREY

had we never loved

Harlequin Books

TORONTO • NEW YORK • LONDON
AMSTERDAM • PARIS • SYDNEY • HAMBURG
STOCKHOLM • ATHENS • TOKYO • MILAN

Harlequin Presents first edition April 1985
ISBN 0-373-10781-1

Original hardcover edition published in 1984
by Mills & Boon Limited

CHAPTER ONE

LINNET gasped and spluttered as her head broke water and she raised a weary hand to push away her black hair which was plastered over her face. The lochside looked as far away as ever and for the first time, she began to doubt her ability to reach it. With the doubt came a weary kind of resignation and the knowledge that it was all her own fault. She was no stranger to the loch, she knew it was tidal—too often in the past she'd swum here, but today she'd been careless, excited and determined to try out her new toy—the light fibreglass canoe which had decorated the roof of her old Mini all the way from Blackpool.

She'd been a fool, watching the tide come creaming in through the narrow sea entrance, battering itself into spray on the rocks before she'd even unstrapped the canoe so that the slack water period was gone and the tide turned before she'd carried the canoe down to the water's edge. And in Lochardh when the tide turned, it did it with a vengeance. The water funnelled out back into the sea, carrying every bit of floating debris with it and that was just what she was—floating debris. The canoe had turned turtle and she'd been spilled out. She should have made more of an effort to right the little craft instead of striking out for the shore. In the canoe she'd have stood a better chance, not much better since she'd lost her paddle, but better than nothing.

She'd heard it said that a person's whole life flashed before their eyes when they were drowning so she supposed she was drowning now—there were pictures flick-flicking through her mind as she tried to make her weary arms and legs obey her. Uncle Fergie was there, very neat and prim in his best tweed suit—just as he'd been when he came to London to fetch her from the Home where she'd been placed when her parents had been killed in the fire which had destroyed her home.

They had said, those anonymous grown-ups at the Home, that they were trying to trace her kinfolk but she hadn't believed them, not until Uncle Fergie came and she'd wept all over that tweed suit which had smelled of strange things—strange to her seven year old mind but which she'd later discovered were peat smoke, strong pipe tobacco and dogs. Dear Uncle Fergie, who'd fed her toffees and chocolate on the train which had taken them from London to Inverness because he couldn't think of any other way of comforting her.

The cold loch water closed over her head again but she hardly noticed, the pictures were flicking by so quickly. Life in Glenardh where Uncle Fergie was factor—the cold winters, the warm, sunny days of the too short summers—the one roomed school tacked on to the chapel and Miss Mackie in her neat Edinburgh suit with the stiff-collared blouse, speaking with her neat Edinburgh accent: 'You should try for a wee bit more work, Linnie and a wee bit less dreaming'; Catriona MacDonald with the flaming red hair working at her loom while her grannie sat silent by the fire . . .

HAD WE NEVER LOVED 7

Sheena and Archie Gow, so alike with their silver fair hair and sea-grey eyes—so unalike in temperament. Sheena, frilly and bossy and Archie thin and pale— hiding behind anybody, even little Linnie Frazer. The pictures changed and Ruby was at the entrance to her booth on Blackpool Prom, standing beside the crudely painted board which said *Gypsy Ruby Lee* and Ruby's voice, strangely deep and harsh for a woman, as she'd beckoned, 'Come inside, dearie, cross my palm with the Old Queen's shilling you have in your pocket.' But how had Ruby known that? It had been Uncle Fergie's lucky piece, all he'd had to leave her except for his few sticks of furniture.

The water wasn't cold any longer—it was almost warm, lapping over her face—filling her mouth and nostrils. Linnet thought she would sleep now, she was too tired to stay awake any longer. Perhaps she'd sleep forever, but Ruby's voice went on and on in her head. *No, lovey—No, my little Birdie! No sleep for you yet. The water signs are bad for you. Wake up, Birdie, wake up!* And over and above all these faces that other face—teak brown under the dark red hair—hard, angry and unforgiving the grey eyes filled with distaste and distrust.

Linnet went slack in the water, her arms and legs heavy—too tired to make another stroke. Why bother? It would all be very painless—no todays, no tomorrows so, when someone tried to pull her head off, she was cross. The pain was excruciating, as if every hair on her head was being wrenched from her scalp. She moaned a protest and the water wasn't warm or friendly any longer. It was cold and it tugged at her slender body angrily as if it was loth to let her go. The fresh wind blew chill on her shoulders and back, there was a rasp of wood against her thighs and stomach and she was face down in the bottom of a boat with a weight on her back which squeezed regularly, nearly crushing her until she vomited.

'Don't you know better than that?' This was a real voice, not one of those she'd been hearing in her mind—a remembered voice—too well remembered. Salt water dribbled from her mouth to mix with the tears spilling down her face and she was at last turned over on to her back to feel the cool sun on her face.

Uncle Fergie faded back into the past—he'd been long gone—he'd died when she was sixteen and Ruby wasn't calling her any more. But Ruby wasn't dead, she was alive, waiting in Blackpool, no longer *Gypsy Ruby Lee—Fortune Teller* with a stuffy, dark little booth on the prom but *Madame Lee—Savante* with a consulting room and a country-wide clientele.

Linnet's black hair dripped cold water on to her shoulders and she shivered as the voice came again with not a shred of sympathy in it, only anger. 'Linnet! Come on! Snap out of it! You're not dead yet!'

Only one person had ever called her 'Linnet', Uncle Fergie had always said 'Linnie' so everybody in the glen had copied him—'Linnie Frazer'. And to Ruby she'd always been 'Birdie', ever since they'd met five years ago. But that other one had always said 'Linnet' and she opened her eyes and squinted up into the harsh, hawklike, teak brown face which was as unforgiving as ever. She drew a shaking hand across her wet mouth and said the first thing which came into her mind in a weak, shaky little voice which gained strength and steadiness as she went on.

'H-him-s-self in p-person! Y-you should t-take lessons in life saving. Y-you've nearly scalped me!' She felt rather pleased with herself about that short speech—after all, Linnie Frazer had always had the reputation of being as tough and hardy as a weed despite her small size. She was still tough and hardy and she'd prove it—even if she was shaking like a jelly inside from exhaustion and fright!

'And you nearly drowned, you damn little fool!' he retorted. 'What did you expect me to do, jump in with you? Next time, I'll use a boat hook, you'll find that a lot more painful.'

She closed her eyes in resignation as she recruited her strength. 'Here we go again,' she muttered savagely. 'Nothing's changed, has it? Himself should have learned by now to control his nasty temper!' She moved her hand and something cold and slimy jerked against it. Now was the time to prove that it took more than a near fatal accident to put her down, not after she'd survived so much in the past. 'Oh lord, Piers; did you have to flop me down with the fish? I'll stink!' And with an effort and a pale attempt at a pert grin, she pulled herself into a sitting position in the well of the old boat and shivered. 'I'd have made it,' she snarled.

'Like hell, you would!' He snarled back at her as he stripped off his guernsey and dropped it across her back. 'You were a goner and I nearly wrecked this boat getting to you. You can thank your lucky stars I was close enough to fish you out before you went down for the last time—and cover yourself up, my girl. What you're wearing isn't decent.'

Linnet looked down at her red silk bikini—French

cut, very expensive and very flattering, but much too revealing for these northern waters. But it was all she'd had with her and she'd covered it with a light nylon jacket which she'd shrugged herself out of when the canoe capsized. She hadn't set out this morning intending to swim in it—it hadn't been designed for swimming in and if she hadn't lost the canoe, it wouldn't even have got wet. Now it was probably spoiled. She put her head down between her knees and muttered, defiant to the end.

'You don't like it? It went down a bomb at St Tropez last year—at least the bottom half did,' she qualified it. 'Topless, you know!'

'That, I could see,' he leered at her. 'The remains of the tan's pretty comprehensive. I'd make a guess and say you didn't wear the bottom half much either.'

'And who's so damn old fashioned he hasn't heard of sunray treatment?' she demanded ferociously. 'They do it in all the best beauty salons nowadays. Eight sessions before you go on holiday—guaranteed to give you a Bahama bronze *all over*!'

His leer disappeared as quickly as it had come and he looked at her as though he didn't believe a word she said. It made her mad and, weakness forgotten, she exploded.

'O.K. Have it your way. I've been strutting around the south of France without a stitch on! That's what you believe, it's what you *want* to believe, you prig!'

'Then keep those fashions for the south of France,' he informed her haughtily. 'We don't want them here!'

'Too inflammatory?' she sneered. Her strength was coming back and with it, her courage so that she could abandon her faking. She raised long, dark blue eyes to his steely grey ones. 'What d'you want me to do about my bikini, take it off? Piers, darling— why didn't you ask? You know I'd do anything to oblige . . .'

'Cover yourself!' He snapped it out at her and at the fury in his voice, she wriggled hastily into the guernsey. It still held the warmth from his body and she snuggled into it gratefully; turning up the over-long sleeves into wide cuffs and pushing the hem down over her hips—it came nearly to her knees, he was a big, tall man.

'Is that discreet enough for you, you narrow minded Hibernian?'

'It's better,' he acknowledged ungraciously, reaching into the cuddy with one hand while he held firmly to the tiller with the other. The hand came out holding a silver topped, leather covered hunting flask which he tossed into her navy blue, woolly lap. 'Drink,' he commanded. 'It'll maybe stop you getting a chill and when you've had a drink, you can tell me what you're doing here.'

Linnet let a very small quantity of the mellow, single malt whisky trickle down her throat. It lodged in her stomach to give her a false sense of well being, and meanwhile she examined him consideringly out of the corners of her eyes, masking the look with the thick fringe of her lashes while she sized up the situation.

Himself, Piers Alexander MacArdh wouldn't be pleased she was here—flapping around once more in *his* bailiwick. He'd very likely hit the roof! He wouldn't look on it as the return of the prodigal and there'd be neither welcome nor a fatted calf. She, Linnet, was persona non grata as far as Himself of Glenardh was concerned. But it was done and there was no way she could see whereby he could undo it. If he didn't like it, he'd have to lump it!

'I've been hiring property,' she answered smoothly, but her fingers were shaking as she recapped the flask and handed it back to him.

'*Not* in Glenardh!' He shot the warning at her and inside, under her insouciant exterior, she cringed at his vehemence. She could still remember the time when she'd have wept if he'd spoken to her like that, but those days were gone—long gone and she was a different person now. The thought didn't comfort her but then, she remembered Ruby—Linnet wasn't alone any more, she had a back-up which put things in a much better light.

'Too late,' she murmured, smiling sweetly. 'The deed is done, you'll just have to be brave and take your medicine—it won't do you any good to lose that famous temper and start throwing things. As of April first, Miss Ruby Lee is the summer tenant of the domain known as Ardh Lodge; comprising the house and outbuildings pertaining thereto and the one acre of land on which they stand.' She pursed her lips judiciously. 'Bounded on the south by . . .'

'. . . Miss Ruby Lee?' His black eyebrows rose in hauteur and his eyes glittered at her. The spring sunlight shone down on his head, turning his hair to the colour of old, well polished mahogany and the sight of it turned her heart to water—just as it had always done. 'Who's Miss Ruby Lee, or is that another name for Miss Linnet Frazer?'

'Tut-tut,' she reproved. 'How could *Miss* Linnet *Frazer* be your tenant? That lady doesn't exist any longer, not in law.' The whisky was giving her an inner warmth and her voice held a jeering note. 'But don't let it worry you, my little Scots Laird—just brace yourself for the worst. Miss Ruby Lee's my employer and where she goes, I go—we're almost like Siamese twins,' and she chuckled softly as she eyed him with sparkling defiance before continuing smoothly.

'The lease is all signed and sealed, right down to your own hallowed signature—not even an anonymous scribble "On behalf of"—so, unless you take yourself off for parts unknown or lock yourself up in one of your turrets, you're going to be seeing me pretty frequently over the next six months. As a matter of fact,' she pursed her mouth again and screwed up her face into a spiteful grimace, 'I was going to call on you later today—to pay my respects to the Laird of the Glen and ask you to do something about your deer fence at the back of the lodge—it's in a poor state of repair.' She gave him a nasty smile, almost a leer. 'And Ruby is delighted with her summer cottage although she hasn't seen it yet—so delighted, you won't be able to budge her so don't bother trying. If you don't like things as they are, you can always emigrate!'

'Me emigrate!' He gave a short, hard laugh with no mirth in it. 'That's a fine way of saying "run away" but it wasn't myself who ran away last time.' He changed back to his jeering tone. 'We're coming up to Eilean Ardh now so get ready to move about, my lass. That's if you *can* move. Let's see if your legs are as active as your poisonous little tongue. You can take the line on to the jetty and make us fast; I don't want this boat joining your canoe at the bottom of the loch.'

Linnet looked ahead. Sure enough, they were approaching the promontory which jutted out where the loch bent round at a right angle. Uncle Fergie had always said this bend was a geological freak, that Glenardh, the whole of it was a freak of nature—a glen where no glen should be, not on this part of the west coast of Scotland. It had something to do with that right angled bend in the loch so that the upper stretches were protected from the fierce westerly winds in winter—that and the Gulf Stream hitting the coast nearby so that the weather was milder. Trees and vegetation flourished, there was very little snow in winter here among the bleakly inhospitable, heather covered highlands. In fact, the glen enjoyed the same climate and conditions as were found a little further north at Inverewe where Osgood Mackenzie had planted his tropical gardens.

'The canoe won't sink,' she disputed aggravatingly. 'So, unless it's been battered to bits on the rocks, it should be on its way to Lewis by now, that's if the currents don't take it down to Skye,' but she obeyed, scrambling to her feet and wiping herself free of fish slime with a grimace of distaste. Her legs still felt rubbery but she compelled them to do what was necessary.

Her leap on to the stone jetty was neither graceful nor very competent, but one couldn't have everything and at least she made it and didn't fall into the loch or slip when she landed on her feet. She felt an imperceptible shiver run down her spine, a shiver which had nothing to do with the temperature or being still shaky and waterlogged.

Eilean Ardh, built on the promontory, on the foundations of an ancient vitrified fort and joined to the lochside by a stout bridge which had replaced the original drawbridge, was an intimidating place. It was too big, too tall, too . . . She searched for the correct word in her mind; too *raw*! Half house, half fortress—the wind-scoured, towering grey walls always made her think of the blood which had been spilled on them over the generations. Clan wars, sea raiders—so many men had died on these walls and at sunset, when the light was rosy over the loch, the walls took on a reddish tinge—they looked as though they'd been soaked in blood.

Her bare foot bumped against the stone bollard and she squealed with pain, hopping and clasping her bruised toes—but she secured the line, after a fashion and Piers stepped ashore, but only after he'd threaded his catch on to thin lines, two of them, to hold one in either hand. She hoped he'd miss his footing and fall into the water with an almighty splash; he was big enough to make a good splash and she would stand and jeer at him while he floundered. She wouldn't even offer a hand to help him out, but hoping wasn't enough—not with an expert like Piers. He made it easily in one lithe leap and stood on the jetty, towering over her, looking down on her from his six foot of height and grinning sardonically.

'That's what town living and high heels do for you,' he glanced down at the smear of blood on her toes with a notable lack of sympathy. 'They make your feet soft!'

'*You* are wearing shoes, you louse!' she spat and then, as he walked ahead, leaving her to limp along behind him, 'Shall I be allowed—will you permit me to go straight through your house and out of the front door to the bridge or would my passing through bring on an attack of the plague?'

Piers stopped, turning to look at her gravely. 'But you said you were coming to see me,' he raised an eyebrow. 'Come in and see me now, it'll save you a journey, but,' his smile became cruel, 'I think I should have my guernsey first.'

'No!' She clutched at the thickly knitted wool, hugging it to her body desperately and with frantic fingers. ' "Louse" is the wrong word for you, it's not bad enough. You've developed into a sadist. I'm not going in there,' she nodded towards the house, 'not in just a bikini.'

'My guernsey,' he was implacable. 'What's the matter, Linnet? You're surely not shy of that sexy little body—you used not to be so, are you going to give me my jumper or do I have to take it from you.'

'You lay one finger on me and I'll—I'll . . .'

'. . .You'll do what?' He was sarcastic and with cause. He could have picked her up under one arm—held her easily with one hand—she just wasn't big enough to fight him. She couldn't even kick his shins, her bare feet would have no effect.

Linnet curbed her temper while she went still and cold—much colder than she'd been in the loch, then slowly pulling herself to her full five foot three inches, she dragged the guernsey over her head and threw it at him to stand defiantly in the sunlight with her head held high. The minuscule scraps of red silk hid so little, but she was determined to show no embarrassment as he laughed down at her and tossed the jumper over his shoulder—— He hadn't wanted it—not to wear—he'd just wanted to humiliate her!

'Follow me if you've forgotten the way,' and he strode off round the low, wide parapet which was all that was left of the high wall which had been Eilean Ardh's first line of defence in the troubled times.

She followed him resignedly, there was nothing else she could do. The only other way off this semi island was to drop over the parapet and scramble, crabwise over the rough rocks until she'd made the half circuit which would bring her out under the bridge close to the lochside, but she'd done that once before and learned her lesson. That time, she'd arrived at the bridge with feet bruised and bleeding despite wearing plimsolls which had been cut to ribbons on the rocks. In bare feet, she'd stand no chance at all.

She looked down at the rocks speculatively, they looked just as lethal as ever, one slip and it wouldn't only be her feet which would suffer—a bikini offered far less protection than the jeans and sweater she'd worn that other time, so she trod carefully along the parapet and finally dropped down into the sunny little courtyard to follow him up the stone steps to the wide open door which led into the back of the buildings. A way which was always used when anybody came in from the loch via the jetty.

The main door which fronted on to the lochside was much more imposing; battlescarred and at least six inches thick, it was too heavy to be opened with ease and somebody had, at some time cut a smaller door in its thickness. Linnet grinned to herself as she recalled the tremendous baulk of timber which slotted across

the width of it—there was no key to Eilean Ardh, only
something it took three men to lift.

Another cold shiver ran down her back as she
stepped into the dimness of a stone walled passageway,
her feet chilling at the touch of the grey stone flags
beneath them. Nothing had changed, but then it
would be difficult to do a conversion job on a building
which had walls nine foot thick. She nodded as Piers
waved her to wait for him and she heard the muffled
sound of voices as he vanished into the kitchens; there
were two of them—one for the family and one where
the food for the rough and scruff had been prepared.
Her mouth twisted into a wry grin as she recalled the
tale of MacNeil of Kismull; how a fanfare had been
blown from the walls in ancient days and the
trumpeter had announced—'Princes and potentates of
the world may now take their meat. The MacNeil has
eaten!' Lord, the airs these little highland lairds had
given themselves!

And then, Piers, minus his fish, was back with her, a
hand on her bare arm to impel her up the narrow,
stone staircase which was built into the curving wall of
a turret.

'So modern and comfortable!' She forced the words
out although her teeth were beginning to chatter and
she was trembling all over. 'My God, this place is a
relic of the Stone Age. You'd be more up to date living
in a broch!'

'Careful!' he cautioned, indicating the steep drop
from the unrailed stairs to the flags of the passageway
below.

Linnet shrugged. She had a good head for heights
but at this moment, there seemed to be something

wrong with her. The paving below did a stately waltz before her eyes and she felt as though every drop of blood had drained away from her heart. Her muscles wouldn't obey her and she raised a face gone paper white while tears welled into her eyes.

'I d-don't feel very w-well,' it came out pathetically in a weak whimper before all her blood collected in her ears to roar madly through her head and she felt herself falling.

When she opened her eyes it was to the bright light of midday. She was lying on a hard, uncomfortable surface, she felt as though she was trussed up like a chicken and her mouth was covered with a thick width of a woolly substance. She wriggled and moved her head until her mouth was free of the blanket which covered it and gave the beginnings of a piercing scream. A large hand with long, strong fingers clamped itself over her mouth and Piers glared down at her.

'Hush!' He commanded her silence irritably.

Linnet hushed, moving her head and wrinkling her nose distastefully. 'What happened?' She could remember the stairs, looking down, the whirl of the paving. 'Did I fall? Ugh! What have you been doing to me? I smell like a distillery.' She eyed him balefully. 'I can't move!'

'Shock,' he answered her garbled questions curtly. 'As for what I've done to you, I've fed you some whisky and wrapped you in a blanket, that's all. You were as cold as death. How long had you been in the water before I pulled you out?'

'It felt like hours, but it couldn't have been very long,' she closed her eyes, feeling once again the pull of the current as it had dragged at her arms and legs. 'It's put me off swimming for life,' she added with a return of courage as she struggled her arms free of the blanket. 'Where's wherever I am?'

'The Room,' he was sardonic. 'An appropriate place, don't you agree?'

'Oh God!' Her eyes slid round, over the bare stone of the walls, the sparse furnishings—a wooden stool, a table and the cot bed on which she was lying. Her gaze slid to the deep set, heavy little door which had a small iron grille set in the top half and then wandered across to the window. It was then that a small fear cramped her stomach.

This was probably the largest window in the castle—a glassed-in aperture nearly seven foot high and three foot wide; starting a foot above the floor and reaching to the cornice of the sloping ceiling. It meant something to her and she cast about in her mind for that something—a wild tale she'd heard years ago when she was small and which still had the power to make her blood run cold.

'Ah, the *Room*!' She was chatty to cover her weak nervousness. Piers couldn't do anything to her—he was modern and civilised, wasn't he? Or was he? 'I think I've heard of this place,' she continued in a high, thin voice which she strove to keep steady. 'Wasn't it where the MacArdhs kept their prisoners—traitors, captured enemies and such? No way out except the window and if they didn't jump after three or four days, they were pushed!' It wasn't a nice thought and her mouth became rather dry.

'Aye,' he nodded seriously. 'But you've missed out on one category. We also punished unfaithful wives in the same way. It's a long way down to the rocks below, although, in the case of a man, he could maybe jump far enough out to miss the rocks and land in the loch.' Piers shrugged. 'Not that it made much difference—he was dead either way—smashed to pieces or killed when he swam ashore.'

'Oh, very feudal,' she complimented him as she huddled back into the blanket seeking some warmth. The whole atmosphere of the room was redolent of a cold, hopeless despair. 'Isn't it a good job we now live in a civilised age?' And she could still hear the high, thinness of her voice as she tried to look unconcerned. 'It must have cost your family a fortune to keep reglazing the window.'

'It wasn't glazed until about a hundred years ago,' his mouth curved into a mirthless smile, 'and I've only regretted the civilising process once.' He stooped over her and she could smell the whisky on his breath. But he wasn't drunk—Piers had never drunk a lot and it never made him bad tempered or unpleasant. Once or twice, when he'd gone over what he called his limit, he'd merely been very happy, but—people change and she hadn't seen him for five years . . .

'Three hundred years ago, Linnet,' he continued in a low growl, 'you'd have gone out of that window and I don't think you'd have been able to jump far enough out to clear the rocks, but I wouldn't have let you crash on them. I'd have put the nets out to catch you as you fell. You'd have had injuries but they wouldn't have been fatal, you'd have lived but I doubt if any man would have wanted you afterwards.'

Linnet did her best not to show fear although it was thick about her, as though the old walls were impregnated with it. 'You're mad!' She raised her chin. 'This isn't three hundred years ago, this is now and you don't push people out of windows nowadays, not even if you don't like them very much,' and she closed her eyes and turned her head away from him.

'But it's more than not liking you very much, my dear,' his fingers under her chin forced her face round without pity or gentleness.

'Oh, I know *that*,' she flicked her eyes open and looked straight into his. 'It's hating me, isn't it? I caught you on your tender spot, I wounded your damn pride and that's one thing you'll never forgive. I humiliated you and you couldn't stand it.' She sat up on the bed, dragging the blanket round her. 'And what are you going to do about it?' she demanded viciously. 'Keep me prisoner up here? You've got a hope! I'll soon be missed.'

'A missing canoe, a missing girl,' he shrugged. 'It rather speaks for itself, doesn't it? Sooner or later, the canoe, or its wreckage will be found—nobody saw me drag you out of the loch, nobody saw you come in here . . .' He didn't finish the sentence, he didn't have to. He simply stood, watching her face, seeing comprehension dawn slowly, followed by an expression of outraged disbelief.

'You wouldn't!' She stared at him and then, not quite so firmly, 'You wouldn't dare.'

'The idea frightens you?'

'Frightens me?' She gave an almost hysterical laugh. '*You* frighten me! I've been almost drowned, I've been in shock and now, you're threatening to wall me up alive in this place. If I turned into a gibbering idiot in front of your eyes, it'd be no more than I expect or you deserve. One of us is demented—every screw loose and I don't think it's me. I *know* it isn't me!' She slumped back on the cot and pulled the blanket closely about her. 'Shock,' she muttered aloud to herself. 'I'm suffering from shock, that's what's the matter. I'm seeing things, hearing things, but they're not real.' She looked around her, studiously avoiding his person. 'I'll wake up in a minute or so,' she added hopefully.

'You're staring a lot,' Piers interrupted her survey. 'What d'you think of the MacArdhs' punishment place?'

'Bloody awful,' she growled. 'Hasn't any member of your family ever gone in for the lighter side of life or are you still stuck in the Middle Ages—and it's damn cold as well. I don't wonder people jumped out of the window rather than stay here. You should jazz it up a bit.'

'There's this,' he crossed to the wall opposite the window and twitched at a piece of faded tapestry which hung there and as he spoke her heart went cold. She didn't need him to show her what was behind the tapestry, she already knew what it covered. She knew as if it was hanging there in the full light of day. She'd seen it once, very briefly before he and his mother had hurried it away, hidden it from curious eyes and she didn't want to see it again, not ever.

'Yes, my dear,' he purred. 'Just as you said, I thought I'd jazz the place up so I had this brought up here.' Another twitch of his hand and the tapestry rattled aside, the big wooden rings clattering on the polished pole to reveal a larger than life painting in an ornate gilded frame. 'I like to keep my memories,

Linnet,' he was sombre. 'I don't run away from them as you did.'

In one swift, lithe movement, or so it seemed to her, he was back beside her, pulling her from the cot with a firm hand under her chin to tilt her face to the painting.

'Look at it, Linnet and remember,' he snarled. 'Remember her?' He reiterated it violently as he shook her. '*Look!* Isn't she beautiful? Every charm displayed for anybody to see! Where would I get a better picture of my blue eyed, black haired slut of a wife?'

CHAPTER TWO

LINNET fought the pressure of Piers' fingers under her chin until she thought her neck would break and then, with a whimper of distress, she gave in—lifting her head to look straight at the portrait—at herself smiling out of the canvas; at the slender, white body, gleaming in the sunlight with only the long black hair to cover it; at the innocently inviting pose, young breasts thrusting and the seductive line of waist, hip and thigh. She looked until it all blurred before her eyes and she closed them on tears.

She had thought she'd been able to put it all out of her mind, that she'd forgotten but it was all as fresh as though it had happened yesterday. Her mouth tortured itself into a bitter smile at the way her forgetting hadn't worked.

After Uncle Fergie had died and the new factor took over the house, Piers' mother had suggested Linnet worked at Eilean Ardh but suddenly, she was sent to the hotel in Creevie—a live-in stand-in for any of the staff who were sick or on holiday. Piers' mother had said it was a better opportunity, that she'd learn more, be better equipped to earn her living, but Linnet knew differently! Piers had started to take an interest in her and that wasn't to be allowed. Piers' future was mapped out for him, he was to marry Sheena—a nice, tidy family arrangement.

But Piers had had a mind of his own, he didn't care

about family arrangements and he'd waited until she, Linnet, was eighteen and then proposed. He'd said he would take her in her shift if she had nothing better. His mother hadn't liked it but Piers was a man grown, not a lad to have his wife chosen for him.

Linnet recalled that walk down the aisle of the small chapel and the way he'd turned his head to watch her coming to him—the light shining on his hair and his grey eyes promising. She'd loved him for so long, ever since she'd been small and at last, her dreams were coming true. But not for long! They'd all come back to Eilean Ardh after the wedding and there were Sheena and her brother, Archie, with their wedding present and they'd pulled off the wrappings right before her eyes.

It was the one time when she'd been grateful to her new mother-in-law, even liked her a little.

'Cover that up at once!' Piers' mother had been rigid with disapproval. 'And take it away. Put it where nobody can see it and we'll have to hope nobody's already had a view.' But it had been already too late, Piers had seen it and his eyes were now promising something quite different.

Linnet wrenched herself back to the present and opened her eyes, uncaring whether he could see her tears or not and with a swift movement of her hand, she pushed his fingers from her chin to stand free of him and swing round. Her eyes were dry now and blazing, but her voice, when she found it, was steady and cool.

'I hope Archie's improved his technique,' she drawled, lowering her lashes to hide the hurt in her eyes. 'He always did have talent, of course, but what's the object of showing me that thing again? Or are you seeing if I've changed in the past five years?'

Her hands swept down, deliberately emphasising the points made in the painting—breasts, waist, hips, thighs—'I don't think it's so much like me any more, except the face. Do you? I'm slimmer now where it matters—my puppy fat's gone,' and with a grunt of disgust, she dragged the blanket about her. 'All right, you've had your bit of fun and I hope you enjoyed it so may I please go?' and she stalked to the door and turned on him once more, mustering a little dignity from thin air.

'It was a *lovely* wedding present, a real surprise so I hope you thanked Archie and Sheena for their kind thought and apologised that I didn't add my thanks to yours.'

'You can go when you're properly dressed,' his voice was as cool as her own. 'Wait here and I'll get some clothes for you.' He pushed her back on to the narrow cot and went out of the door, closing it behind him. She heard the turn of the key in the lock, but the sound didn't amuse her, rather it frightened her. Piers had always had a savage temper and this locking her in, coming on top of his implied threats made her uneasy but . . . She calmed down, forcing herself to be reasonable and put ridiculous, frightening notions out of her head.

But they kept filtering back until her hands were wet with perspiration and her nails were biting into her palms. *Don't think about him* she screamed at herself silently. *Think about something else*, and went forward to take a closer look at the painting. The only other time she'd seen it, she'd been so shocked, so frightened by Piers' hard held rage, she hadn't examined it properly. In fact, she'd taken one quick look at it, another at Piers' white face and shut her eyes before she could scream herself hoarse.

The folds of the blanket tangled about her feet but she lifted them clear and went a bit nearer to get a better view. She knew very little about art, only enough to realise this wasn't a masterpiece; it was competent, no more. There was something about the pose which was familiar and something about the figure which was wrong—the wrongness tugged at her memory but what it was exactly, she couldn't tell. All she knew was that she had never posed for this although she'd seen something very like it somewhere. A girl, up to her knees in the loch, wringing the water from her hair—the connection escaped her and with a sad little sigh, she returned to the cot.

What was the use anyway; Piers believed it was her, painted from life and nothing she could say or do would convince him otherwise. What was the use of fighting when she hadn't a chance of winning?

The turn of the key in the lock and the door opening brought her upright as Piers entered. He put a tray down on the table and handed her the skirt and woolly jumper which he'd been carrying tossed over his shoulder. As an afterthought, he produced some scraps of underwear from his pocket.

'Get yourself into them,' he directed, 'and have something to eat. I've brought some sandwiches and a pot of tea. After that, I'll drive you back to the lodge.' But when she remained still, waiting for him either to go or to turn his back, he shook his head at her. 'I was deprived of the pleasure of undressing my wife so this time, I'll watch her dress. Who knows, I might get some pleasure from that.'

'You bastard!' She was almost crying with rage and humiliation as she clutched the blanket closer about her and gazed longingly at the garments. 'Turn your back if you won't get out,' and at the sight of his unyielding face—'Please!'

'Since you've asked so nicely,' the smile on his mouth was a travesty of humour, it made him look fiendish, 'I'll maybe look out of the window.'

Hurriedly, under cover of the blanket, she turned her back on him to scramble into underwear; a pair of briefs and a slip—she didn't bother with the bra, it didn't look the right size. Five years had made a difference—she might have fined down in some areas but she'd developed a firmer, fuller bosom. She wriggled herself into the skirt which was now too big about the waist and a trifle tight across her bottom and hastily pulled the jumper over her head.

Dressed, she regained some of her *savoir-faire*. 'No shoes,' she complained tartly.

'I couldn't find any,' he snapped back at her. 'Only some silly white satin things.'

'True. I didn't suppose you would,' she answered wearily and with a bitter note in her voice. 'I only had the one pair and I took them with me when I left. Never mind, I've come this far barefoot, I daresay I can manage the rest of the way.' She folded the blanket carefully and laid it on the narrow cot, lifting her chin as she straightened. 'I'm ready now, shall we go? I don't wish to trespass any longer,' and as his eyes slid to the tray, '*No!* I won't eat your salt. I won't be beholden to you. That way

I can be as rude as I like.' And she was violent about it.

'So much modesty and pride,' he jeered. 'A bit belated, don't you think? Isn't it about time you apologised?'

'I don't feel apologetic,' she flared.

'Then you should,' his answer came swiftly. 'As for the other, starve if you wish and when you pass out again, I'll carry you like the good, kind, considerate husband I am. By the way, one thing I've always wondered—how did you get out of the house on our wedding night? I watched for you, I had an idea what was going through your mind.'

'You watched the wrong way,' she answered shortly and refused to say another word. Why should she tell him? So, he'd watched for her, had he? Not when she'd been looking at him, he hadn't!

From the gloom of the gallery, she'd looked down on her own wedding party. It had been a highland wedding, very colourful and the men had been the peacocks—they'd outshone the women.

The recently installed electric lights had shone down from the chandeliers in the big hall, shone on rippling kilts and swirling plaids, the black and yellow of MacLeods, the blue of Campbells, the dark green of Mackenzies, Stewart red, the redder red of MacArdhs. It had glinted everywhere on silver; buttons and shoe buckles, the settings of huge, cairngorm set, plaid brooches and the polished hilts of skean-dhus tucked into tartan stockings.

Sheena had been drifting round in Piers' arms while the fiddles had played a waltz. Archie, drunk as a coot had been leaning against a wall cuddling yet another glass of whisky—as if he hadn't had enough already and she, Linnet, escaping—taking her time and going as quietly and inconspicuously as she could.

Up to the bedroom, ripping herself out of her dress, the dress of which she'd been so proud and which had been totally eclipsed by Sheena's bridal white, Paris model. She'd scuttled about, struggling herself into jeans and a sweater, almost crying when she couldn't find her anorak—slipping her feet into an old pair of plimsolls but having the forethought to collect a large shoulder bag, stuff it with a change of underwear, a skirt, some tee shirts and her purse. She'd slipped the bulging thing on to her shoulders like a schoolboy's satchel and tied her good shoes about her neck by the laces before she'd fled silently down the stairs.

There'd been nobody to see her, they were all having too good a time. It wasn't every day that Himself of Glenardh—The MacArdh Himself was married! She'd gone out by the kitchen door, the same door she'd come in today and dropped over the parapet to crawl, in the dark over the rocks until, at last she'd reached the bridge. After that, she'd changed her shoes, tossing the ragged remains of the plimsolls into the loch where she hoped they'd float out on the morning tide and then limped away. Up through the glen, over the pass at the head of it and down the winding mountain road to Creevie where she'd waited outside the small town and hitched a lift with an early lorry going to Inverary.

'You didn't go out through the main door,' he interrupted her memories.

'No,' she was serene. 'I went through the kitchen

door and over the rocks to the bridge. It made a mess of my feet but it was worth it.'

Piers wasn't sympathetic, but then she'd never expected sympathy from him. She wouldn't have accepted it if he'd shown any. 'All to escape from me!' He raised an eyebrow. 'Anybody'd think I intended to be a brutal husband.'

'And of course, you didn't,' she growled. 'It was all going to be sweetness and light, love evermore with a little kind understanding thrown in for a bonus, wasn't it?' And with her nose in the air and her back as straight as a ramrod, she swept past him to the door. He followed her and as he closed the door behind him, she breathed a little sigh of relief. For a few moments in that room, she'd been nearly paralysed with terror—the layer of modern, civilised behaviour tended to be very thin on the Celtic race.

At the end of the bridge, she halted and Piers, walking behind her had, perforce to halt as well. 'Thanks,' she was prim and chilly. 'This is as far as you need to come. You've seen me off your property and you needn't fear I'll ever set foot in your house again. Wild horses wouldn't drag me here!'

'Don't be a sulky little fool, Linnet,' his hand in the middle of her back pushed and she stumbled forward on to the rough surface of the unmade road which skirted both sides of this end of the loch. 'You've more than a four mile walk to the lodge, or have you forgotten it's on the other side. Here,' he practically frogmarched her to where a battered Landrover was parked. 'Get in and I'll drive you.'

'So much thought for my well being,' she snapped back at him. 'When what you'd really like is to get me in the loch and hold my head under until I stopped breathing!' She scrambled into the high cab and settled herself, inwardly tense but outwardly serene. 'But I can do with the lift,' she admitted graciously. 'I went for my paddle before breakfast and I'm beginning to feel empty. What time is it now?'

'About half past two,' he started the engine and the Landrover bumped off down the road. 'It was probably a good thing you hadn't eaten though, you'd have been much sicker after swallowing all that water.'

The jolting ride stopped any form of conversation and Linnet's thoughts took a different direction to arrive at a conclusion which filled her with satisfied malice so that halfway, just as they were crossing the narrow bridge which spanned the stream tumbling down from the hills at the head of the glen, she laid a hand on her husband's arm.

'This is going to make things a bit difficult for you,' she announced with spiteful anticipation and her mouth curved into a gleeful smile. 'I only arrived yesterday and so far, I've not seen a soul from the glen although I did a bit of shopping and had a meal in Creevie on the way in. The news will soon get around and your damn pride's going to take a wallop! Me at the lodge and you, in Eilean Ardh—People will remember the wedding and start talking, surmising. It won't bother me of course but your face is going to be red.'

'And just for that,' he stopped the Landrover, jumping down to come around and open the door for her, 'you can bloody well walk the rest of the way, Mistress MacArdh. My face won't be red but yours might because I'm going to leave all the explanations to you. Your brazen looks and your snappish tongue should get you out of most corners.' He swung her down, climbed back behind the wheel and drove off in a squeal of gears, leaving her with at least two miles of rough road to cover barefoot.

Linnet watched the Landrover snarl off, back along the road it had come and with a shrug, she turned and picked her way ahead in the early spring sunshine. Another example of Piers' temper, and she had hoped he might have it under better control nowadays. At thirty two, or was it thirty three, he should have learned to crowd it down, not let it run away with him—not go off the deep end at the drop of a hat. That temper, was it one of the reasons she loved him? She put her head on one side and considered while she dropped on to the grassy verge and nursed her sore feet.

There were so many reasons why she loved him— she couldn't remember a time when she hadn't. Ever since she'd been a ten-year-old kid and he'd been nearly a man, coming home from university during the vacations and dazzling her poor, childish mind. Puppy love? She didn't think so; more like a slavish devotion which she'd never grown out of, but had grown into concealing and she'd been nearly eighteen before she hadn't needed to conceal it any longer.

'I've been waiting for you to grow up, Linnet,' he'd said. 'Have you grown up enough yet?' And after that, everything had been so certain, so right! Piers hadn't given a damn about the penniless orphan thing, he'd haunted the hotel in Creevie where she worked and he'd ridden rough shod over his mother's wishes and objections . . .

With a squeal of brakes, the Landrover stopped alongside her once more and Piers was out of his seat, his arms were around her and he threw her into the passenger seat like a sack of potatoes. Then he slammed the door on her with a curt 'Get in!' which wasn't necessary because she already *was*—and as he heaved himself back into the driving seat, 'Damn you, Linnet! Why did you have to come back? What in hell am I going to do with you?'

Linnet retreated behind her only defence—her outwardly cool, unemotional detachment. 'Ignore me,' she advised, 'as I shall ignore you.' The detachment had come in very useful when she'd been younger and ever since that dreadful wedding day with its abysmal failure of an ending, she'd worn it like a cloak. Her mind went back again—Sheena and Archie had intended to make a public display of that painting; she supposed she should have been more grateful to Piers' mother for preventing that . . .

'Your mother?' She made the enquiry calmly. 'I heard in Creevie that she'd left the glen.'

'Edinburgh,' he was curt. 'She always hated it here,' he swore vitriolically under his breath. 'What have we got *now*?'

Linnet looked through the windscreen at the little scene under the pines by the lodge gate. Two men in smart green overalls were seated at a small table under a tree, playing cards and drinking canned beer, while in the background a furniture van was parked.

'A few extra things Ruby wanted,' she kept it cool. 'A special table, a couple of more comfortable chairs, an orthopaedic mattress, a desk for me—things like that. I'll have to see to them at once, the men have a long run back.' The Landrover slowed to a halt and, disdaining his help, she swung herself down to look up at him. 'Thank you for the lift,' her lips smiled while her eyes remained blank and dead—but as he made no move to leave, 'There's nothing further for you here, Piers so don't waste your time.'

But Piers wasn't to be dismissed so easily, she should have known that and she should have got out of the way in time before he swung down and literally pinned her against the side of the Landrover, out of sight of the furniture men.

'Dinner tonight,' it wasn't an invitation, it was a command and when she stiffened at his peremptory tone and looked suspicious, 'No, not at Eilean Ardh. We'll go to the hotel in Creevie.'

'To be seen by all and sundry?' she raised a haughty eyebrow. 'A face saving operation?'

'Exactly,' he grinned down at her wolfishly. 'But your face, not mine,' his eyes were as blank as her own, they gazed down at her from a bleak, expressionless face, saying nothing—only holding a chill danger in their depths. Linnet tried to control the little shiver of excitement which ran down her spine but it was uncontrollable and she lowered her lashes in case her eyes gave her away.

'We'll carry this off with a high hand,' Piers made it sound so easy. 'Himself on one side of the loch and Herself on the other,' it was almost a sneer. 'You've misjudged the grapevine, my little dear. The word's out already I think and people will be wanting to know what comes next so we'll give them a little something to be going on with.'

'You disappoint me!' She put her head at a defiant

angle and grimaced a smile. 'A Hero and Leander situation—are you going to refuse to swim the Hellespont? Yes,' at his frown, 'I can see you are.' She pretended to study him clinically as though she would know what made him tick. 'I can't think why you bothered to haul me out of the loch this morning, if that's the case.'

'Then you should remember the MacArdh motto, Linnet. "What we have, we hold",' he was brutally cruel. 'Even when, or if we don't want it any more!'

Linnet felt the blood drain out of her face and she closed her eyes before he could see the naked pain in them. 'That's putting it in a nutshell,' she murmured while she thanked heaven that she didn't normally have a high colour. Nobody ever noticed when she lost what little she had. 'I must remember not to put a lamp in my window to guide you. But if, as you say, you hold on to what you have, why have you leased the lodge?'

'Because I was tired of tourists thundering on my door, wanting to buy or lease—and I was tired of my factor's disapproving face when I refused the offers he sent me. We both knew I needed the money but I didn't want open air barbecues and pop music under my nose so, I told him to lease but only to a certain type. Your Miss Lee seemed to fit the bill but now, I begin to wonder. You can tell me more over dinner tonight.'

So, that explained his invitation, or had it sounded more like a royal command? Linnet stamped off without a backward glance although her dignified retreat was rather spoiled by the stony soil beneath her bare feet. She only just took in his 'I'll call for you at eight.' And she didn't turn her head when the Landrover roared off. Instead, she concentrated on the furniture men who had, by this time, secreted the pack of cards and were busily unloading the van and while she directed them, apparently intent only on what she was doing, her mind was indulging in mental gymnastics.

Tell him about Ruby? That ought to make his hair curl, especially if she made it the whole truth. The little dark booth on the prom, the old gypsy woman in her frowsty black dress—her over abundance of clanking bracelets and fake jewellery and the so obviously dyed hair. Everything had been so garish that Linnet had been reluctant to even step through the doorway. She had no money to waste on such nonsense and the booth smelled of stale air and fish and chips. She would never have entered except for Ruby's sharp little black eyes which had seemed to have an almost hypnotic effect on her—that and the uncanny thing about Uncle Fergie's old shilling piece.

But once inside the booth, Ruby hadn't told her fortune. Instead, from beneath a rickety table she'd produced a thermos of nearly black tea and two thick mugs while she told her own.

'A change coming for me and a little bird to bring it,' the old woman's eyes had glittered with satisfaction. 'D'you mind if I calls you "Birdie", dear?'

'My name's Linnet,' Linnet had corrected her.

'Same thing,' Ruby had looked pleased. 'I'm never wrong with the Tarot cards, I saw you coming, I knew you was for me,' and she'd waved Linnet's objections aside with a jangle of bracelets and the dull gleam of several rings which pretended, not very successfully, to be diamonds. 'And you're looking for work,' the black eyes had bored into hers. 'You work for me, my Birdie. There's work and money for both of us, the cards said so.'

And out of sheer necessity—Linnet had barely enough left to pay for another night's lodging, she had accepted. After all, her wonderful dream of happiness and love had turned sour on her, it had turned out to be more of a nightmare than a dream and it didn't matter much what happened to her now. So, she'd put herself and her future in the old woman's hands and accepted the job together with a mugful of strong tea.

No, she decided, she wouldn't tell Piers anything but what was strictly necessary. There were times, like now, when she was apart from Ruby that it all seemed unbelievable. Yet people—wealthy, well known people, came for help to 'Madame Lee—Savante' and kept coming back, again and again. Satisfied customers, Ruby called them. Ruby, with Linnet's help had changed her image; she still wore black but it was no longer frowsty, it was haute couture. The bracelets had disappeared together with the fake diamond rings. She still wore rings, not quite as many, but real and she'd stopped dying her hair so that nowadays it showed its true snow white. Ruby had also taken elocution lessons and moved her centre of operations from the booth on the prom to the sitting room of a luxury flat in the best residential area of Blackpool. Taken all round, Ruby had become a great success, she only had one drawback and she wasn't shy about it—she could neither read nor write.

'Too late to learn now, Birdie,' the old lady had cackled with laughter when Linnet suggested lessons.

'Besides, now I got you,'—the elocution had a habit of slipping in private—'I don't need to, do I? I got me witch ball and me Tarot cards, that's my area. I leaves the reading and the writing to you.'

Piers would never believe that Ruby was anything but a charlatan and could she blame him when a lot of the time that was what she believed herself and as she hurried through her dressing for dinner at the hotel, adjusting the coral pink, silk two piece and finding a lipstick to match it, Linnet made up her mind to phone Ruby from the hotel. Maybe she'd even ask her what to do. If Ruby's advice was good enough for business men, stockbrokers, theatrical producers and the stars of stage, cinema and T.V., it ought to be good enough for Linnet Frazer!

Most of Ruby's advice was sheer common sense anyway and Linnet suspected that she herself had gone far beyond the point where she could trust her own. One look at Piers, one touch of his hand and she couldn't even trust herself. This was her personal act of defiance, having dinner with him—afraid and yet unable to refuse. She glanced at her watch—there was still time to be sensible—take off her dress, lock the doors and go to bed. But she knew she wasn't going to be sensible. Her hand quivered as she outlined her lips delicately, but whether it was from fear or excitement, she didn't care to guess. The answer might not be to her liking!

At last, satisfied with her appearance, Linnet went downstairs. It was going to be the most disastrous evening, she knew it. Perhaps, after all, she ought to undress, go to bed and ignore his knock but Piers wouldn't be put off so easily. If she locked the doors, he'd find some way in if he had to smash a window to do it and saying she was too tired or had a headache wouldn't work either.

With a little sigh at her own weak stupidity, she examined herself in the mirror once more. She *did* look rather nice—the pink silk was flattering to her rather sallow complexion, her hair was a straight, glossy fall of blue blackness and her mouth, now that it was lipsticked didn't seem so vulnerable. 'Courage,' she told her reflection. 'He can only insult you and what's that to you? You've been insulted by him before, it won't be anything new and he can't do much in a crowded hotel dining room.'

CHAPTER THREE

PIERS arrived outside the lodge at precisely eight o'clock which was neither more nor less than Linnet had expected—punctuality was one of his virtues. He had also put clean seat covers on the Landrover and Linnet, who was particular about where she sat in her best clothes, beamed with delight. This amount of consideration, she decided, deserved something better than an icy approach but an icy approach was about as much as she could manage and finally she lapsed into silence since Piers was as withdrawn as she.

The hotel in Creevie looked very much as it had done when she had worked there so that although she knew none of the staff, she felt quite at home in the dining room among the green plush, the polished mahogany and the tartan overtones; apparently the new proprietors had a liking for Victoriana. Linnet avoided sitting against a background of tartan wallpaper which would have killed her coral pink stone dead and chose instead a table by one of the mock gothic windows from where she could count the mounted antlers and other trophies of the chase which were mounted on the walls.

Their waitress recommended the traditional Scottish meal, a speciality of the house and Linnet dined well, if not too wisely on smoked mackerel fillets, an enormous steak of Scottish beef with all the trimmings and finished off with a desert of raspberry shortcake drowned in cream. The other diners were obviously either tourists or dedicated fishermen—she thought she heard an Edinburgh accent and perhaps a Glasgow one while a couple of ladies sounded so obviously English that it hurt—which made her feel safe. The last thing she wanted or needed now was an encounter with an old acquaintance from the glen who would regard her with a speculative eye before rushing home to debate and redebate the past. In her mind, she could hear it.

'The MacArdh was at the hotel with Herself! Just as if nothing had happened! Lovely they looked together—Perhaps . . .' and it would all be in the precise, almost unaccented English of people to whom the Gaelic was the first language.

She stole a glance at her husband—he *did* look lovely. His hair, smoothed down for the occasion glowed as deeply as the old fashioned mahogany sideboards; his white shirt was crisply white and his well cut, well worn tweed jacket made him look bigger and broader than ever. He had a free, uncaged look about him—overlaid by a veneer of civilisation, but it was there—like a disdainful eagle looking down on a covey of plump, silly partridges. His kilt rippled sinuously about his lean hips and her heart squeezed painfully as her sharp eyes noted the tiny, incredibly neat darn in the cuff of his shirt. Money was far from plentiful in the glen and a small smile touched her lips as her eyes went back to the kilt.

It had probably been his father's, kilts were handed down from father to son to grandson as long as there was any life left in them and hard tartan lasted for ever. She'd seen a kilt in the Highland Museum in

Fort William which had been over a hundred years old
and yet looked as good as new, the tartan still firm and
strong and the colours fresh and bright . . .

'Linnet,' his voice broke in on her musings. 'I'll ask
you for the third and last time: tell me about Miss
Ruby Lee.'

Linnet brushed away her spasm of silly tenderness
and her eyes sparkled with resentment. Damn the
man, he was going into his 'Laird of the Glen' act—
assuming that Ruby wasn't a fit sort of person to live
in his poky little lodge, that she had to be vetted
before he could accept her! Ruby—her friend, who'd
given her help when there'd been nobody else to turn
to.

'Ruby?' She said the name gently and her lips
curved into a smile. 'She's more than my employer,
she's my friend.'

Piers was harsh. 'That's no recommendation—in
fact, quite the reverse!'

'Maybe,' Linnet's mouth, neither as soft or gentle as
it had been five years ago, hardened into a thin,
straight line of temper. 'But what's that got to do with
it?'

'Just this,' Piers leaned back in his chair, long
brown fingers fiddling with the stem of his wine glass.
'I rang Murdo, my factor, this afternoon after I got
back from dropping you off and he tells me the lodge
was hired unseen, that your Miss Lee has never laid
eyes on it. From that, I'm led to suppose that it was all
your idea.'

'Wrong again,' she gave him a pitying smile. 'I had
nothing to do with it. Ruby saw your ad. in the paper
and it was all her own idea. She's hired your lodge for

six months and I consider she's paying you very well for the privilege. Everything's been signed and sealed so isn't it rather late in the day to start letting your scruples show? And, knowing Ruby, I don't think she'll let you get away with tearing up the lease or anything like that—not without some pretty hefty compensation. If you insisted, you might find yourself right in the middle of an unpleasant and expensive lawsuit and,' she let her eyes roam over him insolently. 'I've this idea that while Ruby can afford to go to law, you can't!'

'Then tell me, where did you meet her.'

Linnet gave a crow of bitter laughter which successfully banished any tender feeling she might have left for him. 'When I left this place,' she decided not to pull any punches, 'I had to find work and somewhere to live and I had to do it quickly because I didn't have much money. I decided to go to Blackpool, I'd calculated that was the furthest I could afford to travel so . . .'

'. . . Why Blackpool?'

'Because, my dear innocent, it happens to be a resort. You know—stuffed full of boarding houses and hotels—all I knew at that time was hotel work and I thought I'd stand a better chance of getting work there . . .'

'Then Miss Ruby Lee either runs a boarding house or an hotel?'

'No,' she grinned defiantly in his face. 'Nothing like that at all. You're way off beam.'

'How old is she?'

'How rude can you get?' she spat back at him. 'Let's say she's too old for you. As for how old, I've no real

idea. Maybe sixty, maybe seventy, maybe even older—
I've never presumed to ask.'

'Hmm!' he snorted down his long beak of a nose. 'I
can hardly be blamed for thinking that leasing my
lodge was your idea,' Piers made it sound like an
accusation.

'Which just shows how stupid you are,' she fired up
at once. 'D'you think anything, and I mean *anything*
would have made me come back here of my own free
will? Make me choose any place within a hundred
mile radius of you? Because, if you thought that, you
flatter yourself. Of inclination, I'd rather have gone to
the other end of the earth. All I ever wanted to do was
to forget you ever existed and,' her tone changed to
one of grumbling disgust, 'I was doing a bloody good
job of forgetting until Ruby got this bee in her bonnet.
If you want to know the truth, I tried to put her off
and that reminds me, she *must* have a telephone. I
know you're wired up here, but when I tried Telecom
yesterday they were awkward about it. They say they
need your permission to put up an extra pole or
something.'

'So they do,' he nodded. 'Why d'you want a phone?'

'Oh, for crying out loud,' she snapped. 'I've just
explained, if you'd only listen. Ruby's an old lady—I
might need a doctor.'

'Which is quite reasonable,' Piers was graciously
bland and it set her teeth on edge. 'I'll see about it
first thing tomorrow morning. Now, tell me some
more about Miss Ruby Lee—you say she doesn't run
an hotel or a boarding house—are you listening to me,
Linnet?'

'Sorry,' she stirred her coffee while she thought of

what to say and suddenly, it came to her—the truth, nothing but the truth, but not the whole truth—'Ruby's a professional woman, a consultant. She's semi-retired now, only taking a few cases, interesting ones—which is another reason for wanting a phone,' she added. 'And you needn't be afraid she'll want to tear up and down the loch in a speedboat or give wild parties with fairy lights strung in the trees. Oh heavens!' She gave a squawk of dismay. 'It's past ten o'clock and I ought to ring her, but before I do, are you satisfied? Ruby lives a very quiet life, very private and I promise that I, personally won't obtrude. You'll hardly know we're there.'

'Don't be a bigger fool than you can help,' Piers was harsh and she glared at him. She wouldn't try to be pleasant any more! He could like it or lump it—she didn't care and the less she saw of him the better! And she flounced away to the public phone in the foyer, the pleated skirt of her coral pink silk dress flirting about her long, slender legs.

''Lo, Birdie. I was just drinking me cocoa. Has my stuff arrived? 'Ave you got everything fixed up for me?' Ruby's deep voice came over the wire, clearly and comfortingly.

'Everything in apple pie order.' Linnet found herself smiling fatuously at the receiver. She couldn't help it; it felt so wonderful to be talking to a friend—to be able to say anything she liked without having to weigh each word before it was released from her lips and then, she looked up and scowled at Piers where he was lounging against the wall, close by the big plastic bubble which was supposed to guarantee the caller complete privacy. 'I'm just waiting for you,' she told the receiver with an expression of longing. 'Are you ready to leave yet? Shall I come down this weekend to fetch you?'

'No,' Ruby was definite. 'Not this weekend or the next. You'll have to give me a couple of weeks before I can get away, there's a lot to do. Lor'! I didn't realise how easy you made things for me and there's a few letters to see to. Tell you what, you send me one of them cards with the number on it soon's you get the phone in. I can do numbers so I'll ring you and tell you when to come. Another thing I been thinking about, that little car of yours. 'Tisn't going to be big enough, not for all my stuff so I been talking to that young man from the garage. He says they've got a second hand Range Rover coming in and it'll be just the sort of car we want so I've got first refusal on it . . .'

'A Range Rover!' Linnet's voice squeaked with surprise. 'But darling, they cost the earth, even second hand and they're very . . .'

'. . . I can afford it so don't you worry,' Ruby interrupted before Linnet could say that like the Landrover, the Range Rover was very high, not built for old ladies, but Ruby continued remorselessly. 'You ain't lonely up there, all on your own? And don't forget that card—I'll put the letters in one of the envelopes you left me and post them on. Ring me as soon as you can,' and with a grunt of satisfaction, Ruby hung up.

Piers was back at the table when she returned from the phone, the bill was paid and her eyes widened as she caught sight of the total. But it was no use offering to pay her half even though she could well afford it, she knew that and besides, he was looking grim. He'd evidently decided he'd wasted enough time on her, extracted all the information there was about Ruby, so now, he wished to terminate the encounter. And that was all right by her! He rushed her through her coffee, which wasn't difficult, it had cooled while she was on the phone and she was hustled out of the dining room and through the car park at something approaching the speed of light.

Piers tossed her up into her seat as though she weighed no more than a feather, slid into his own and the Landrover started off. He treated the long, curving climb from Creevie to the head of the pass as though it was part of a racing circuit and he took the narrower, more winding road down to the glen at a speed which, if anybody else had been driving, would have made her hair curl. But with Piers, she always felt safe, he was neither careless nor reckless. If he went fast, it was because he knew he could. He knew every twist and turn of these roads like the back of his hand.

Past Glenardh village, where the tarmac surface ended, the Landrover was sent thundering along the unmade, rutted road like a bucking bronco and Linnet slid a swift glance at her husband's face. She couldn't see much in the dim glow of the instrument panel, but what she could see was enough to confirm what she had suspected from the taut atmosphere which seemed to surround them. Piers was in a black rage about something and her heart beat a little more quickly as she went over all the events and conversation of the past few hours.

Until he'd started asking about Ruby, there'd been nothing—but nothing—to account for his change of mood. He'd been quite—quite civilised and good tempered while they'd been talking about people and places she'd known as a child. Even when they'd talked about her employer, it had all been very innocuous—she'd given truthful answers—insofar as she'd thought it wise and he'd accepted what she'd told him—even seemed satisfied with it . . .

She gave up and, in the darkness, shrugged her shoulders. So! He was upset about something—let him be upset and in a temper—it had nothing to do with her so there was no need for her to feel guilty.

The Landrover came to rest outside the lodge with a screech of brakes; it stopped so suddenly and so violently, Linnet was flung forward against her safety belt, but once she'd overcome the initial shock, her own temper rose. 'What d'you think you're doing?' she yelled. 'You could have killed us!'

'Don't tempt me,' he snarled back in the darkness and was out of the vehicle and round to her side before she could get her breath. Her door was flung open and she was half hauled, half carried from the seat and after being set on her feet, towed through the wicket gate and up the garden path to be dumped at the door while he threw it open with a crash which nearly set it off its hinges. With a hard, painful hand in the small of her back, he propelled her into the living room where he switched on a table lamp and pushed her roughly into one of the newly delivered chintz covered chairs.

'So, that's the sort of talking you do to your *employer*,' his voice and his eyes were deadly. 'You're not bringing your fancy man here, my girl—not while you're still my wife and never, if I have anything to do with it!'

Linnet ignored the first part—she hardly heard it, being fully occupied with getting her breath back and retrieving a bit of dignity after his rough handling. But the second part came over loud and clear so that when she raised her blue eyes to meet his fearlessly, there was an almost vicious expression in their depths. Never had she been treated like this—*never*, and she wasn't going to stand for it!

'Your wife!' She gave a shrill trill of high, almost hysterical laughter. 'That's a laugh! Who was it wouldn't dirty his hands with a slut like me? Who said I'd defile his bed? Who was it told me the only place he'd have me was in the straw? I'll tell you who!' She paused for breath while her fingers crooked into claws. 'Oh yes, I'll tell you who said all those things—it strikes me you *need* having your memory refreshed. It was my dear husband, of course! *You!* Grrr!' She snarled it all out between set teeth. 'My husband, the man who has suddenly remembered he's my husband after conveniently forgetting the fact for five years! You never gave a damn about me, I could have starved for all you cared and it's no thanks to you I didn't!' She ended on a sob, took a deep breath and started all over again on an even higher note. 'I wasn't good enough for your High and Mightiness—you *spurned* me!' Her hysteria mounted. 'You threatened me,' and as his mouth opened to make a retort, she went on swiftly, giving him no chance to interrupt. 'You *frightened* me, I *hate* you!'

As her rage increased, so his seemed to lessen and he produced the flask from his pocket and thrust it into her hands. 'Stop behaving like a heroine from a Victorian melodrama,' he admonished in quite a normal voice, 'or I'll treat you like the child you seem to be. I'll put you over my knee and slap you till you can't sit down for a week. Take a drink of that,' he nodded at the flask, 'I said take a drink from it, *not* throw it at me—and start behaving like a normal, human being. We've a few problems to iron out and we'll get nowhere if you're going to be hysterical. I said only that I wouldn't have you bringing your lover here and I meant it. I'll see you both in hell first—or at the bottom of the loch!'

'M-my lover?' Holding on to the remnants of her sanity with a tremendous effort, she managed to put the flask down on a small table instead of throwing it at him. 'You, you . . .' her voice started to rise again and she stuttered with rage. 'You know nothing of my lovelife and it's none of your business anyway.'

Linnet forced herself back to normality, relaxing her hands and when she judged she could speak without screaming, she raised a haughty eyebrow. 'What gave you the idea I'd taken a lover, may I ask?'

'You did,' Piers had himself well in hand now. His rage was still there but he had it under control. His eyes glittered and there were white patches at the corners of his mouth and at the base of his imperious nose, but the tone of his voice was almost conversational. 'You phoned him tonight from the hotel and you had the gall to do it right under my nose.'

Linnet, who was far from cool herself, stopped being afraid, only her anger remained. 'I phoned Ruby,' she corrected him coolly, 'and might I remind you that private phone calls are supposed to be just that—private! You had no right to come snooping, listening to what I said.'

'I have a perfect right,' his coolness matched her own. 'The best right in the world. You're my wife . . .'

'. . . so good of you and so thoughtful to remember that,' she cooed spitefully but he ignored her interruption as though she hadn't spoken.

'. . . and don't try to tell me you were phoning your Ruby!' he snapped. 'Girls don't call their employers "darling", not if that employer's an old lady—nor do they smile idiotically at the phone while they're speaking to "her". I'm not a fool, Linnet, so stop treating me as one. I'm beginning to think . . .'

'. . . Oh lord, save me from a man who thinks . . .'

'. . . beginning to think you're up to something—all this is coming out too pat,' he went on like a tank, flattening her feeble interruptions, rolling over them regardless. 'I lease a house and a bit of land to a Miss Ruby Lee but it's you who arrives here and you have a glib explanation but no Miss Lee. You say she's coming later and you interrupt dinner to phone her. You call her "darling", you say you're "just waiting for *her* to arrive"—you make comments about the price of a car which "she" intends to buy—not the sort of car an old lady would like and all the time, you're smiling as though "she" was the light of your life . . .'

Linnet tried to take lessons from him in the art of producing a reasoned argument—she tortured her face into what she hoped was a copy of his coolness—his damned superiority.

'And you'd like to think the worst, wouldn't you? What story would satisfy you, I wonder? Miss Lee's a man and I'm his mistress but don't you think that's a bit involved, specially as it's only to get a six months lease on this little house—are there any other reasons festering away in your evil mind?' She paused for breath and he took advantage of the pause.

'I don't have an evil mind!'

'You don't? You could have fooled me!' and she continued swiftly in case he broke in on her again. There were a lot of things she wanted to say to him and they were arranging themselves in her mind. She wanted to get them out into words while they still made sense. 'Who else but somebody with a rotten, lousy, evil mind would take one look at a painting and decide that I'd posed for it? Who else would immediately assume that I'd gone to bed with the artist and as for your latest, all I can say is that solitude's gone to your brain; you've gone stark raving mad! Or—,' her eyes slitted and her smile became meaningful in the nastiest possible way.

'Is it the other way round?' she demanded silkily. 'Hasn't it been so solitary after all? Could it be you're trying to get rid of me because of something *you've* done? I'm sure Sheena offered you a little consolation when you "found out" what a naughty girl I'd been. Did you take her to bed on our wedding night? I'm sure she wouldn't have refused and it wouldn't have turned *her* into a tramp, would it? After all, you might have been having second thoughts about all that lovely money she has, regretting you'd settled for a penniless nobody.' Poison dripped from her tongue in a not very well reasoned argument and she was proud of it. Proud too of the steadiness of her voice and the fact that she could control her tears and was ready with another tongue lashing if he made one more unpleasant remark concerning her motives or her morals.

But Piers was too swift for her, he abandoned the verbal argument and he was standing over her, his hand fastened into the front of her coral pink silk before she could gasp. She was hauled bodily to her feet and his arms were about her and his mouth savagely on hers which put a temporary end to her defiance. This was what she wanted, what she'd always wanted but—not this way—not in anger. She gave a little moan of despair and pain—Piers wasn't only angry, he was furious—as he'd every right to be and he wasn't letting her fight free of him, not even to get her breath.

It was true, what he'd said of her, calling her a slut—she was. *His* slut and she always had been, ever since she'd been old enough to know what life was about. Any time he'd wanted her, with or without love, he could have had her—she'd have given herself willingly—only he'd never asked that of her. Instead, he'd been very correct and when they'd married—fool that she'd been, she'd thought she held heaven in her hands. But her bright world had shattered before she'd even had time to feel it properly, the pieces falling through her fingers. And what was worse—there'd never be another man for her—only him!

Dizzily, she could feel herself responding as the savagery went out of his mouth. His hands no longer hurt her and a bitter sweet passion grew between them. She clung to the last vestiges of her control as she felt her breasts harden under his searching fingers. With a soft sigh, she relaxed against him, her mouth opening under his and it was just as it had been before they married. When he'd been tender and considerate of her ignorance, leading her gently, sweetly along a way she didn't know and for one delicious, rapturous moment, she was content; pressing herself against him until fear of the unknown made her hesitate.

The Cinderella story wasn't for her and her Prince Charming was no knight in shining armour, he was only a man filled with rage and distrust. Even though she ached for him, she knew there was no bright future for her in this embrace. He'd only despise her more and she'd have to run away again.

Why, oh why had Ruby picked on this particular house in this particular place? Why couldn't it have been somewhere else, some other world? Hadn't she been hurt enough? Slowly, very slowly because she had to force herself every inch of the way, she brought her hands from where they were caressing the back of his neck and pushed them firmly against his chest— making her lips cold and lifeless under his while her heart wept.

'I don't respond to mauling,' she croaked bravely when at last he raised his head. She refused to meet his eyes and dropped back in the chair to contemplate the ruin of the coral pink two piece. The little jacket had escaped unharmed but the bodice of the dress was ripped and several buttons were missing.

'And I prefer a more civilised approach,' her voice sounded quite normal and steady and she wondered how long she could keep this up. Sitting here, behaving as though nothing out of the way had happened, as though she was used to being mauled every day of her life. 'Please don't apologise,' she muttered in a bitterly humorous tone. 'I'm sure you wouldn't mean a word of it.' Her voice babbled on and she couldn't stop it. 'The Stone Age is obviously your scene but I don't consider our sterile marriage any reason for you to behave like Neanderthal Man!'

'Linnet,' Piers was breathing as fast as she was and there was a flush on the high bosses of his cheekbones. He tried to pull her back into his arms, 'You talk too much,' he muttered huskily. 'You always did.'

Linnet fought off his hands while she found her breath and her pulse steadied from its hectic thudding. The idea crept into her mind that she might never be normal again, but she sat quietly, avoiding his eyes and her hand reached out for the flask on the table. She poured a good dollop into the silver cup, downed it in one go, gulping as though her life depended on it and being very pleased her hand was steady as a rock.

'Linnet,' Piers stooped over her, grabbing at the flask just as she was about to pour herself another drink. Her eyes sparked with anger—she *needed* that second drink and he was taking it away from her!

'Linnet,' he repeated. 'We have to talk. There are things we have . . .'

'. . . Talk!' she broke in, making a disgusted face at him. The one drink had been sufficient after all—she could feel alcoholic courage coursing through her veins. 'It's no use talking to *you*! You and your double standards—this morning you were getting hot and bothered about a perfectly respectable bikini—tonight, you maul me and try to tear my clothes off. Look what you've done to my dress.'

'. . . and you asked for it, you silly little bitch . . .'

'Oh,' she broke in brightly. 'You mean when I

suggested you'd consoled yourself with Sheena?' She snorted down her small, straight nose. 'You should have married her as your mother planned—that's why she was brought here from Edinburgh—so you'd marry her. Everybody knew that so, why didn't you, instead of sniffing round me. It would have saved a lot of trouble and don't you dare call me a silly bitch— I've eyes in my head and I kept them open even when I was a kid. That's another example of your double standards.'

'What is?' He interrupted her silkily.

'You know!' Her face flushed with embarrassment. 'You and Sheena—the time you took all day and half the night to inspect a deer fence . . .'

Piers surprised her with a soft chuckle. 'It was a very long fence,' he murmured with a reminiscent look in his eye.

'And the time you and she went fishing and missed the tide?' Linnet raised an aggravating eyebrow. 'What was it happened to you? Oh, I remember; you ran the boat on to the sands at Gairloch and you had to wait for the tide to float you off . . .' She snorted again, this time with patent disbelief.

'Jealous?'

'No, I am *not*!' She was furious. 'But me, I wasn't even given a chance to defend myself. I was judged, found guilty and condemned without a hearing and you, my dear husband, you made yourself judge and jury. Now you go back to your house, sit in your famous Room and every time your equally famous temper cools, you can pull back your bit of motheaten tapestry and take another look at my infamy.' Her voice nearly broke on that last word and suddenly, all her temper was gone. She was bone weary, too weary to care any longer.

Leaning back in her chair, she closed her eyes and waited for him to go, but there was no movement. 'Get going,' she muttered sullenly. 'I've had a very bad day. I've been half drowned, frightened out of my wits and I don't think I can take any more. Apart from that, *you* are the one person I can do without,' and she didn't know whether to be glad or sad when she heard the door close behind him but she listened carefully to his footsteps on the path, the click of the gate, the engine of the Landrover coming to life and then, the diminishing sound of it as he drove away.

Like a zombie, she climbed the stairs and stood at the window of her bedroom which overlooked the loch, eventually spotting the gleam of the headlights on the opposite shore. They travelled at what seemed to her to be a snail's pace towards Eilean Ardh. They looked a long way away—a lifetime away.

When Ruby eventually arrived, perhaps it would be better not to go into any explanations—just hand in her resignation and leave without giving any particular reason. It would mess up all Ruby's plans for the long holiday she'd been promising herself, which wouldn't be kind for whatever Ruby was, genuine psychic or charlatan, her 'work' exhausted her. Linnet debated finding another companion, a sceptic, like herself. In her mind, she could hear Ruby's old, deep voice.

''T'wouldn't be a good thing for you to believe— they'd be taking us both off to the funny farm.'

Linnet abandoned planning for the time being. She undressed and showered before she flopped down on the bed, shivering with a kind of pain she'd never felt before. Running away the first time had been bad enough, never mind repeating the performance. She wasn't a child or even a young girl any more and it seemed the older she was, the bigger the loss, the more unendurable the pain. She writhed with it and with the knowledge she'd brought it all on herself.

Piers still wanted her, that had come over loud and clear. It had been there in the sweet savagery of his mouth, the hot glow in his eyes, the warmth of his hands and the thrust of his body against hers. So why did she have to be so damn fussy about the quality of that wanting? Did it really matter that what he was offering wasn't love? Wouldn't a sensual satisfaction be enough for her—easily accomplished and as easily forgotten? Or would that be another thing she wouldn't be able to forget?

She wrapped herself in a robe and went down to make herself some tea.

CHAPTER FOUR

Next afternoon, just as she had finished eating a meagre lunch, the telephone engineers came, making very little fuss and hardly any mess. Her surprise at their promptitude was countered by the information that 'The Forestry Commission had lines everywhere—it was just a matter of connecting to a junction.' They'd already planted their one necessary pole so they installed the instrument, tested it and were gone before she could offer them a cup of tea—to leave her wondering what she could do with the rest of the day.

With grim determination, she avoided looking at the other side of the loch while she made her own tea, which she didn't want and didn't drink, before slipping an anorak over her jeans and sweater and driving into Creevie. Here, she posted the telephone card to Ruby, the code and number printed in big black letters so that the old lady wouldn't be confused and then she raided the newsagent for all the available papers and magazines with a couple of paperbacks added for good measure. The newspapers would come in very useful—Ruby always liked to have a breakdown of the stocks, shares and the money market.

Again, she smiled to herself as she went into Creevie's one and only tea shop. Ruby didn't depend entirely on what her crystal ball and her Tarot cards told her, especially when it came to giving advice to businessmen. For that, she relied for the most part on her own shrewd common sense and the trends given in the financial pages of the daily press. Linnet made a summary every day and read it out to her and Ruby remembered every detail. In common with most illiterate and semi-literate people, her powers to retain the spoken word bordered on the fantastic.

Linnet was on her third scone and her second cup of tea when Sheena Gow came to take the opposite seat at the small table and although the sight of Sheena's silvery fairness and tall, slender elegance set her stomach churning, Linnet schooled her face to an expression of polite, if unenthusiastic recognition. She finished buttering her scone and waited patiently for the first broadside. It wasn't long in coming!

'Little Linnie,' Sheena's accent was a parody of Miss Mackie's neat, Edinburgh Scots, overlaid with the broader, longer vowels and the less precise consonants of Private School English. 'What a surprise to see you here!'

'I'll bet!' Linnet said it under her breath and remained silent while she took stock of Sheena. They had never been very close acquaintances, Sheena was nearer to Piers' thirty-two or three years than to Linnet's twenty-four and besides, Sheena had always held herself aloof from the children in the glen—she was aloof now, under her pleasant exterior; a little more *soigné* perhaps and her sea-grey blue eyes were harder. Linnet took a swift glance—Sheena's eyes were as cold and unwelcoming as the waters of the loch in winter—she was still the Ice Queen, her very white skin never allowed to see the sun—laughter and frowns forbidden to her smooth face for fear they might leave a permanent wrinkle; an elegant package, but one which looked as though it had come direct from a deep freezer. Linnet sat, as taut as a fiddle string while she managed to give an impression of being completely relaxed—smiling at nothing and waiting.

'You're the last person I expected to see here,' Sheena was forced to take the initiative. 'I didn't think you'd ever want to come back.'

Linnet swallowed a mouthful of scone and raised an eyebrow. 'Now why would you think that,' she murmured, deliberately adopting the soft speech of the glen.

Sheena pursed her lips before she gave a small, brittle laugh. 'Perhaps because I remember things so well, Linnie. Correct me if I'm wrong, but you *did* leave under something of a cloud, didn't you?'

'I did,' Linnet made no attempt to deny anything. It wouldn't have been any use, Sheena had been there—she would have still been there when the disappearance of the bride was discovered at last. Instead, she raised her long, dark blue eyes, as hard as Sheena's own and her soft mouth was tight with remembered wrongs. 'And,' her voice was as hard as her eyes, 'I don't need to tell you who was responsible for that "something of a cloud". But that was all a long time ago,' she continued smoothly. She was no longer in awe of Sheena and five years with Ruby had vastly improved her self confidence. She didn't in the least mind about making a scene in public if she felt like it or was driven to it.

'You still blame my poor brother Archie?' Sheena registered sorrow.

'On the contrary,' Linnet reached for her fourth scone, 'I never blamed Archie, but let's not talk about that. Five years is five years and I've learned a lot in that time. I've grown up. After all,' she shrugged, 'one can't go on being an innocent for ever, eventually one learns how to tell the sheep from the goats,' and she thrust out her small chin belligerently.

Sheena backed down as Linnet had thought she would, changing the subject swiftly. 'Piers was telling me over the phone that you've leased the lodge for the summer.'

Linnet poured herself another cup of tea and looked across the table thoughtfully. She'd worked out long ago exactly who was to blame for the debacle of her marriage. The culprit was sitting opposite her, icy eyes glittering in a face which was composed in lines of aloof superiority, like a well bred racehorse regarding the antics of a young donkey. Linnet could understand Sheena's machinations—she'd been brought to Eilean Ardh when she was young and painstakingly groomed to be Piers' wife. Completely sure of herself, Sheena had never envisaged anything going wrong with the plans the family had made for her—so she had felt quite justified in throwing a spanner in the works and the spanner was to hand in the person of her younger brother, Archie. Linnet wondered what plan Sheena was following now, her arrival was no chance thing.

'Not guilty about hiring the lodge,' she smiled across at Sheena. 'I don't have that sort of money. It's my employer who's leasing. She's been looking forward to a long summer holiday, she hasn't had one for ages and I'm just getting things straight for her.'

'Then you won't be staying?' Linnet watched as

Sheena visibly relaxed, it made up her mind for her. She was definitely *not* going to run away again. Maybe she'd get hurt, the hurt had started already, but she'd not be driven out a second time.

'Oh yes, I'll be here,' she murmured with a composed little smile 'My employer needs me. This is all strange to her—hiring a house . . .'

'And at a give away rent,' Sheena deplored. 'I told Piers, he could have asked twice as much, but you know what an old softie he is.'

Linnet didn't know anything of the sort. She probed bruises, the mental ones and a couple of physical ones she'd collected when she'd tangled with him yesterday and she winced inside while remaining outwardly phlegmatic. 'Piers isn't that old,' she pointed out judiciously, 'and as for him being a softie, that can't be true surely? He's made of reinforced concrete!'

'But still capable of being hurt,' Sheena answered Linnet's smile with one of her own—straight out of East Lynne—faint but tragic. 'I suppose it's no use appealing to your better nature, Linnet? You're putting him in a very difficult situation, you know. Just imagine what the people in the glen are saying now you've come back and you know how whispers get around. Don't you think you ought to leave as soon as possible and save everybody a great deal of embarrassment?'

Linnet almost said the wrong thing—almost did the wrong thing. Like hooting with laughter and telling Sheena it was quite impossible to embarrass Piers. She nearly tied her tongue in a knot in order to stop the jeering laugh and the words coming out. Instead, she decided on the practical approach.

'I can't,' she murmured. 'I work for Miss Lee. You don't know much about working for a living, do you? One gets paid for obeying orders and Miss Lee demands obedience in return for paying me a good salary . . .'

'But I'm sure she would understand once the position was explained to her,' the waitress came bustling up and Sheena waved her away with an autocratic hand while she concentrated on her argument. 'Perhaps, if I had a word with her—one business woman to another so to speak? I don't want you to think I'm trying to tell you what to do, but this dreadful mess does need clearing up—it's so embarrassing for all of us.'

'For all of *us*?' Linnet cocked an eyebrow. 'You mean I'm embarrassing you as well as Piers?'

'All of us,' Sheena made it sweeping. 'Piers' family, the people of the glen and yes, since you insist, me! To be blunt, over the past five years, Piers and I have reached an understanding,' the cold, grey-blue eyes were lowered and Sheena contemplated her well cared for hands with every appearance of coyness. 'I like to think I understand Piers better now than ever before. He's the sort of man who can be taken advantage of, you know—he has such funny, old fashioned ideas—almost Victorian. You may not want to believe this but he's always flatly refused to divorce you—every time the subject's come up, he pushes it aside with an excuse that, at the time, you were very young.'

'Perhaps he expected me to divorce *him*,' Linnet widened her eyes until they were like round pools of dark blue. 'That's the Victorian attitude, isn't it, but are you sure we're talking about the same man? The Piers you're describing, the one with old fashioned ideas—full of chivalry and all that rot, I don't think I've ever met him but we all see our fellow men differently, don't we? Perhaps Piers is all things to all men or women,' and she raised her eyebrows impertinently.

Sheena ignored the impertinence—from the tightening of her lips, it cost her a considerable amount of effort—her eyes grew harder until they looked like polished grey stones, but apart from these small signs, she controlled herself beautifully. Her voice, when next she spoke had the tone of one dealing with a mentally disturbed delinquent—she soothed and reasoned.

'You don't know Piers as well as I do, Linnie—after all, I was brought up with him. His mother brought us, Archie and I, here nearly twenty years ago—we all lived together at Eilean Ardh and in nearly twenty years, one learns a lot about a man—talking out problems when they arose . . .'

'Problems like me?'

'Yes,' Sheena nodded in gracious agreement. 'We had a family conference about you, the same as we had about any other thing which had to be decided. It was always the same, we all sat round a table and talked it out.'

Linnet shook her head. 'Too easy to explain it that way,' she murmured. 'What you mean is you ganged up on whichever one of you thought differently and I suppose you nagged away until whoever it was gave up in despair. The wonder to me is that Piers ever managed to get as far as the altar . . .'

'We could hardly stop him, not after he'd told us . . .'

'Told you what?'

'That he *had* to marry you, of course,' Sheena looked pitying. 'I realised then it was inevitable—not what his family had planned for him—and although we tried to tell him he was doing the wrong thing— that neither of you was really to blame, especially you, Linnie, you were hardly more than a child at the time, he simply refused to listen. That's where his old fashioned ways really showed themselves—he kept saying you and he *had* to get married and the more we pleaded with him, the more obstinate he became. What happened to the baby, Linnie?'

Linnet sat quietly while she absorbed the shock and waited for the red mist of rage to clear from before her eyes. At last, it went and she found she could speak normally as she lowered her eyes and concentrated on her fingers, willing them not to turn into claws. 'I never speak of that period of my life,' she murmured. 'It was too distressing.' And Piers, she vowed silently would be distressed when she got her hands on him! She would rend him tooth and nail, she would flay him alive with her tongue—How dare he tell his family a thing like that, the rotten liar!

'I'm sure it was distressing,' Sheena was all sympathy as if she was comforting a pregnant housemaid. 'Did you have an abortion?'

Beneath her lashes, Linnet's eyes gleamed with malice. Two could play at Piers' game. 'I was alone in the world,' she murmured with dramatic pathos.

Sheena became even more sympathetic, wallowing in what she thought was Linnet's grief. 'Yes, my dear, I understand—but so much better, don't you think?'

Linnet watched her fingers move, the sight fascinated her. Everybody in the world had gone mad, including herself—the only sane things left were her fingers which were fumbling in her bag for her purse. She watched them drag it out—she wasn't willing them to do it, they were working quite independently. They sorted among the notes, selected one and then poked about among the small change for the balance of her bill. They even pulled out a couple of extra coins for a tip!

She stood up like a mechanical doll, smiled a mechanical smile and walked across to the cash desk where she paid her bill before going out into the afternoon sunlight.

Driving back from Creevie, she tried studiously not to think about anything. She concentrated on her driving, which wasn't the easiest thing in the world to do when her mind was full of bloodthirsty punishments which she wished to visit on her husband's head—not to mention a host of question marks. What was going on between Piers and Sheena? Why had Piers made his family think she, Linnet, was in the family way?

Such a silly thing to do—that sort of thing didn't matter in the glen—people there looked at that sort of thing differently—a legacy from the days when the glen was remote—when weddings and christenings had to wait on the infrequent visit of a priest . . . The nearside front wheel mounted the grassy verge and brought her back to the present so she put it all from her mind and settled dourly to getting to the lodge in one piece.

Once there, she garaged the Mini and went straight to the outhouse where the fuel for the cooker was kept and savagely smashed up several large chunks of wood, using a sharp little axe and every bit of power in her arm. The result was a pile of chips and splinters which weren't fit for kindling so she kicked them aside and stormed back to the car to collect her reading matter and the few groceries she'd bought.

Eating was out of the question, the scones and the tea in Creevie had taken the edge off her appetite so she made herself a pot of tea, took a couple of aspirin for the headache brought on by too much thought and went upstairs to lie down.

It wasn't her intention to sleep, she'd fully decided to have a sane and sensible think—decide what to do— but halfway through a long speech, carefully composed and diligently rehearsed wherein she tendered her resignation to Ruby without exactly saying why, Linnet became too tired to think any more and her eyes closed.

A sound woke her much later. The sun had long since set and she was surrounded by a pitch dark, moonless night as she lay perfectly still, waiting for the sound to be repeated. She sighed with relief when it came again—the crunch of something on the shingle of the lochside. At least it wasn't somebody in the house. Five years of city life had rearranged her ideas of security, but once back in the glen, she had fallen into the old ways again—not locking doors or even fastening windows—unless it was raining, she didn't even bother to close them. But there was a stealthiness about these night noises which made her wary.

She analysed the small sounds; a boat being hauled up on the shingle, somebody walking across the band of it which lay between the sand and the rocks, then silence until she heard the soft click of the wicket gate ... Linnet threw herself from the bed, pulled a towelling wrap over her underwear and sped downstairs without switching on a light. There was only one person she could think of who would have the cheek, the bloody nerve to walk about, acting as if he owned everything he could see and, arming herself with a stout, ram's horn headed walking stick from the stand in the miniature hallway, she waited behind the unlocked, unbolted front door, the stick ready and poised to deliver a smashing blow just where it would hurt most!

'Naughty!' Piers had outsmarted her by going round the house and coming in through the kitchen door, which was also unlocked. He reached out and caught the ram's horn headed stick and with a swift twist and jerk, her first line of defence was in his hand. In the darkness, she gave a shriek of pure temper and leapt at him, her fingers crooked into claws and aiming for where she judged his face would be.

The resultant scuffle was undignified and as far as Linnet was concerned, humiliating. Coming in, as Piers had from the darkness outside, his eyes needed no period of adjustment whereas she, still muzzy from a heavy sleep was far from her best. The nails of her right hand made contact, she heard an 'Ouch!' and then she was unceremoniously bundled under his arm and carried, kicking into the living room where he switched on the light and nearly threw her in a chair.

'It's worse than trying to catch a wildcat,' Piers mopped at his scratched face and surveyed her grimly while, from under her lowered lashes she watched his every move, searching for some weakness. No kilt this time, only a pair of old and faded jeans which did little to hide his masculinity, and the guernsey pulled over his wide chest but he looked tidy and fresh which was more than could be said for her. She became aware of tumbled, untidy hair, eyes which were still clouded by sleep and a towelling robe which wasn't doing its duty. Swiftly, she pulled it together, belting it firmly before she combed her fingers through her shoulder length, black hair, pushing it away from her face and tucking it behind her ears. She would have liked the opportunity to wash the sleep from her face but he was standing over her, ready to stop her slightest move.

'What fairy tales have you been telling Sheena?' he demanded fiercely.

Linnet summoned up a sidelong grin and deliberately relaxed. 'Only what she expected,' she drawled impertinently while her eyes measured the distance to the door and she calculated her chances of reaching it before he could stop her—they were slim but maybe worth a try... 'In any case,' she continued aggravatingly, 'it was Sheena's fairy tale, not mine. I only added a bit of embroidery.' Her eyes slid once more to the door as she reckoned up the risks.

'Don't try it,' he caught her glance and advised grimly against any attempt to escape. 'I'm in no mood for games.'

'Neither am I,' she became haughty. 'Might I point out, you're here without an invitation—on Ruby's property, where you've no right to be. If this is the way you're going to behave, I shall lock all the doors in future. I think you're carrying this "Laird of the Glen" thing a bit too far.'

'You do that,' he threatened, 'and I'll break them

down!' The lamplight glinted on his reddish brown hair and brought out the harsh planes of his cheek and jaw. 'And you can forget nasty remarks like "Laird of the Glen"—you know it doesn't mean a thing nowadays—nobody pays any attention to it any more.'

'Oh,' she was pert. 'I know it and I suppose most of the villagers do, it's you who doesn't seem to have realised it—strutting around and making up your own rules as you go along.'

'Which is better than making up fanciful stories to mislead people,' he snapped. 'If you had an abortion, you little tramp, it wasn't *my* child!'

'No it wasn't,' she agreed dulcetly, 'and I didn't! But Uncle Fergie always said it was rude to contradict one's elders and betters.' She raised her eyes to the ceiling as though the wonder of it was too much for her comprehension. 'How swiftly news travels—I suppose Sheena was on her way to your place when she met me in the tea shop. Is she staying with you? Now *that* has possibilities, don't you think? No need to make up "fanciful tales" about deer fences or getting stuck overnight on Gairloch sands—not now your mother's taken to living in Edinburgh. I think I may have grounds for divorce—real ones—not the vague incompatibility reason. All I need is some concrete evidence of adultery . . .' She was jeering.

'Which you haven't got,' he jeered back.

'No,' she admitted with a sly smile, 'but I think I could get it. I'm sure the lady would be only too willing to oblige, in fact she'd probably cooperate like mad, but let's get one thing straight—the abortion idea wasn't mine at all, you take the blame for that! Sheena told me all about the family conference when you discussed *me* with your relations. How dared you even suggest you *had* to marry me!' But her words were lost on him, he was gazing at her absently—he was plotting to circumvent her just for the hell of it. She almost hated him for that—almost, but not quite. She loved him far too much ever to be able to hate him properly. If only she could get into his mind—see and understand what was going on behind the expression-less mask of his face.

Apparently, he'd come to some decision for he leaned forward and grabbed her, hauling her out of the chair and tucking her wriggling body under his arm. His hands weren't gentle and she squawked with temper.

'What d'you think you're doing?' she demanded furiously.

'Putting a spoke in your wheel,' he replied and as she struggled, his free hand swiped at her rear. 'Sheena's staying for a few days and I'm supplying her with a chaperon.'

'You can't *do* this,' she protested, still wriggling to be free. 'I won't go, so there!'

'Yes, you will,' Piers was cheerful. 'You'll damn well do as you're told for once.' He set her on her feet and commenced carefully to remove the wide leather belt about his waist, grinning at the fright which showed itself in her steadily widening eyes. 'I'm not going to beat you,' he assured her, 'although I've reason enough. I'm just going to keep you quiet while we get across the loch and into the house.'

'I'll scream my head off,' she threatened, 'and you won't be able to keep me in the boat. I'll jump . . .'

'Scream away,' he was unconcerned. 'There aren't many to hear you and if they do, they'll think it's an owl or a vixen—they'd be right about the vixen—and as for jumping,' he seized a mohair rug from the back of the couch and dropped it across her shoulders, 'you jump and we'll both get wet because I'll fish you out if it takes all night.'

He held her firmly while he arranged the folds of the rug about her and swiftly buckled the belt about her waist, pinning her arms to her sides within the covering, like an ill tied parcel, but leaving her head and face free.

'That should do it,' he sounded satisfied as he slid his fingers under the belt to test its tightness. 'I should have done this years ago. It's the only way to deal with a wildcat like you.'

'I'll show everybody my bruises,' she threatened. 'I'll scream blue murder . . .' The rest of her threats were a muffled mutter as he resignedly pulled a fold of the rug over her face and head.

'Be quiet!' He shook her. 'I'm tired of the sound of your voice. Now, will you walk or do I have to carry you?'

Linnet fought impotently against the rug and belt, she couldn't get free of them so she decided to be as awkward as possible. Never would he be able to say she'd cooperated, not even in the smallest thing. She let her knees buckle and her whole body go limp as she collapsed into a huddle on the floor.

'That's better,' he chuckled and it made her madder than ever so that she wanted to bite him. 'You couldn't have walked anyway, not without something on your feet. Don't you ever wear shoes?' and he picked her up and slung her over his shoulder while keeping a firm grip about her knees.

'You can't,' her voice came muffled from the folds. 'I haven't any clothes . . .'

'. . . but tonight, you won't need them,' he slapped at her rear again but it was only a warning tap, it didn't hurt. 'Tomorrow morning early, I'll row across and pick up what you need for a couple of days.'

'Ruby might ring,' she reminded him as he let himself out of the front door into the dark, quiet night and when he'd closed the door behind him, she heard him shout with laughter.

'Let her ring,' he didn't care about anything or any excuse she could make, she could tell that from the tone of his voice. 'She'll soon get tired of ringing when there's no reply.'

From within the folds, mercifully muffled, she chanted what she thought of him and his high handed ways—none of it good and most of it unprintable. His grip about her knees tightened unmercifully.

'You can stop that foul mouthed stuff,' he warned. 'If you say one more bad word, I'll beat you!' and she was jogged across his shoulder until she thought there'd be no breath left in her body while he crossed the stones, the shingle and the sand to the boat where he dumped her unceremoniously on the wet sand as he pushed the craft into the water. He came back for her and deposited her, not on a seat but in the bottom of the dinghy, between his feet and he took up the oars with a gay whistle as if this was something he did every day—kidnapping unwilling women. Linnet blew the hair out of her face and glared upwards in the darkness.

'As soon as I'm free,' she threatened, 'I'll scratch your eyes out! You'll be sorry for this, you'll see!'

'Linnet,' his voice came from above her, slightly breathless with the effort he was making at the oars. He sounded more amused than angry. 'If you behave yourself, stop being a termagant, you shall have my bed all to yourself . . .'

It was a lifeline and she grabbed at it. 'You mean that? You're not going to—to . . .?'

'Ravish you? No, not if you behave and do as you're told,' there was assurance in his voice and she began to feel more confident. 'Otherwise,' and some of her new found confidence evaporated fast, 'I'll join you and make a night of it. Are you going to behave?'

'Y-yes,' it came out sullen and reluctant, but she agreed.

'And play the loving wife at breakfast tomorrow and whenever I ask?'

Linnet squirmed, trying to find a more comfortable position and the rug eclipsed her face once more. 'Yes,' she mumbled into the folds, grateful for small mercies. A night in bed with him would be too much for her to bear, he'd kiss her stupid and do what he liked with her afterwards and she'd give herself away. She'd be mindless and willing—he'd make a meal of her. The past was hard enough to forget as it was without adding that to it. He wouldn't be kind or gentle, he might not notice it was the first time for her . . .

The dinghy bumped against the side of the jetty and she felt it rock as he jumped out and there was his hand on the belt, hooking into it and hauling her up like a fish on a line. 'Behave?' He stood her on her feet while he tied up the dinghy.

Mutely, she nodded and she was swept up and carried into the house. Not up the back stairs this time—she counted his paces—too many for just crossing the back hall. He was going down it, through to the front of the house. She waggled her head free of the enveloping folds and looked about her.

There wasn't much to see in the dim light from the top of the stairs, but they were the main stairs, proper stairs of wood, not stone and there were sturdy, carved balusters all the way up the smooth curve, surmounted by a wide, shining rail. These were the stairs she had run up the night of the day she was married—at least, he wasn't taking her to the Room. She'd have gone mad in that grim place!

His mother had given her a small bedroom to change in on that dreadful wedding day but Piers wasn't going that far along the gallery. The small room had been right at the end whereas he stopped at the first door to press down on the handle and let them in. There were logs burning in the wide stone fireplace and he set her down in the middle of the hearthrug to undo the belt about her waist. She shivered as the rug fell from her shoulders.

'Cold?'

'No,' she shook her head, her hands, stiff from disuse going to feel down her back. 'Wet! That cockleshell leaks and I've been lying in a pool of water. Talk about the Perils of Pauline—being kidnapped is *not* my idea of fun!'

'Strip off and get into bed,' he suggested. 'You can have my pyjama jacket . . .'

'. . . I'd rather have a hot bath . . .'

'. . . Only under supervision,' he retorted. 'I'm not

trusting you yet, you passed the basic test of escaping from Eilean Ardh.'

'Oh please, you *can* trust me,' she gripped her bottom lip between her teeth to stop them chattering. 'Piers, I give in. I'll do a deal with you. In return for a hot bath and a sandwich, I'll give no trouble. I'll do just what you want, I know when I'm beaten.'

Half an hour later, clean, dry and tucked up in a huge bed which would have held a whole family, never mind a married couple, she took bites from a thick, beef sandwich in between sips from a glass of hot milk liberally laced with whisky. Her courage and self confidence had come back in a rush and she was chatty—or perhaps it was the whisky which was loosening her tongue.

'What's the drill?' She made the enquiry with a conspiratorial grimace. 'How long do I have to playact?'

'Didn't I say?' he shook his head at her. 'A couple of days should do it,' he'd seated himself on the side of the bed, facing her.

'And you also said I could have the bed to my-self . . .?'

'Mmm,' once more Piers nodded. 'The bed, Linnet but not the room. I'll manage on the couch by the fire for tonight.' He waved her ready tongue to silence. 'I shan't disturb you but you'll know just where I am—that I haven't gone looking for comforts elsewhere . . .'

'And you've never done that, have you?' she was waspish.

Piers stood up, pulled a plaid from the clothes press and commenced to wind it round himself before he settled on to the couch beside the fire. In the dimness, his voice came wearily and with the flat ring of honesty.

'Five years is a long time, mo creadh and I never took vows of chastity.'

CHAPTER FIVE

A BAR of bright sunlight shining across her eyelids woke Linnet and she growled—rolling over in the wide bed and trying to find peaceful sleep again. The lovely, never-never land where there were no problems, no heartbreak, only a sweet balm to cover her hurts.

But it was gone, driven away by the sunlight and she was awake to the 'life is real, life is earnest' thing and the hours of daylight loomed ahead of her with danger signals all the way. She opened her eyes and sat up in the bed to find herself alone in the room. Piers and his plaid had vanished, last night's fire was a pile of cold, grey ash in the hearth, but he'd kept his promise—her two suitcases were standing by the side of the bed.

And this morning would be a time for diplomacy, she wrinkled her nose at the thought. There would be Sheena to be faced across the breakfast table— questions to be answered—it wasn't going to be easy. For a moment, she regretted her too ready tongue— everybody had always said it would get her into trouble one day and they'd been right! Trouble was here and now! If she'd only had the sense to be diplomatic last night, she wouldn't be in this position this morning, but had she shown sense? No, she hadn't! She'd allowed her tongue to run away with her, behaving like a tempestuous, belligerent teenager—too intent on inflicting as much pain and distress as possible—as if, in some way it would lessen her own pain.

The bathroom beckoned and she inspected her badly treated towelling wrap ruefully. A big patch on the back was stained and stiff with salt water and sand—that made two garments Piers had ruined for her, but discarding the overlarge pyjama jacket in which she'd slept, she shrugged herself into the wrap and pattered off down the gallery to the bathroom. The place smelled of Sheena's eau de cologne—Chypre—and with a grimace at the pungency, she threw open the windows to air the room before she drew her own bath.

Back once more in the bedroom, she turned her attention to the matter of clothing herself. It was no use trying to compete with Sheena, who always wore classic, elegant skirts and twinsets teamed with the de rigueur pearls—her own chain store skirts and jumpers would suffer too much when compared with hand woven tweeds and cashmere so, defiant to the last, she struggled into a new pair of jeans and a sloppy sweater, the jeans stiff and very tight to compensate for the sweater's sloppiness. And she dragged her hair back ruthlessly into a tight ponytail which made her look as though she'd been scalped.

Despite her deliberate slowness, she found herself hurrying guiltily down the staircase not to keep anybody waiting and she glared at Piers where he stood waiting at the bottom.

'I wasn't going to run away, Mr Gaoler—sir! How did you sleep on that couch—you slipped a disc, I hope?'

His mouth quirked up at one corner and his heavy lidded eyes gleamed behind their fringes of long, curling lashes. 'I managed but I'll admit to a desire to share the bed after an hour or so—and not only because it *was* a bed . . .'

'You should sharpen up a claymore and put it down the middle,' she interrupted. 'That's what they do in all the best historical novels.'

'Claidhiamh mor,' he corrected her pronunciation although to her, it still sounded like one word.

'That's what I said,' she nodded brightly. 'Claymore! I haven't the Gaelic, as you very well know. Uncle Fergie always said you had to take it in with your mother's milk.' She pushed her hands into the hip pockets of her jeans and raised a rather worried face to his. 'How are you going to explain my being here? I hope you haven't been mentioning the unmentionable.'

'You mean "reconciliation"?' Something in the tone of his voice made her look up quickly to find him openly laughing. 'No, my dear, as a matter of fact, I've said nothing except that you were staying here for a few days . . .'

'And of course,' she eyed him darkly, 'nobody would dare to ask you why, would they?'

'Nobody has, so far,' he admitted, 'I can be very off-putting when I put my mind to it, but it's you I'm worried about, you never could carry things off with a high hand. There's a trick to it—you look down your nose as though there's a very bad smell some- where . . .'

'If anybody asks me,' she broke in on his nonsense while she attempted to look down her own nose disdainfully, 'If anybody asks me why I'm staying here, I shall say I'm doing it for sheer spite!'

Breakfast was in a small room to the right of the bottom of the staircase and Sheena was already there, seated behind an enormous coffee pot and smiling her usual cool smile which only just flickered about her lips.

'Good morning, Linnie,' she said it as if it was a daily occurrence, as if there was nothing strange or unusual about Linnet's presence on Eilean Ardh. 'I hope you're feeling better this morning. I wasn't at all surprised when I arrived here to be told you'd already gone to bed, you weren't looking at all well when we met in Creevie. Do you get these attacks often?'

'She's a martyr to them,' Piers caught the conversational ball and kept it rolling smoothly as he passed round the filled coffee cups. 'I've known her spend two whole days in a darkened room.'

Linnet, not to be outdone, seated herself sedately, giving what she hoped was a carefree trill of laughter. 'You're exaggerating, Piers. A day maybe, but never two. As a matter of fact, I feel so much better, I think I'd better go over to the lodge and get on with some work . . .'

'Which I forbid!' He said it lightly enough but beneath the table, his knee pressed against hers warningly. 'You been doing too much rushing about recently and I want you to have a few quiet days here before you dive back into the rat race again. I'm inclined to think that what happened last night was a warning of worse to come so you ought to be careful and not push your luck!'

'And you could be right at that,' Linnet gave him a

wide, meaningless smile as she muttered it under her breath. He'd made his threat in such a nice way— anybody listening would think he was a truly caring husband, but she'd caught the glint in his eyes. He'd meant exactly what he said and it wasn't a thoughtful suggestion, it was a command—she wasn't going to be allowed to backslide, not if the near wolfishness of his caring smile meant what she thought it did.

The door opened and Mrs Matthieson, the housekeeper, entered with a large dish of bacon and eggs to augment the porridge and toast already on the table. Linnet controlled her first impulse to cry 'Matty, how nice to see you again' and contented herself with a gentle smile. The look she received in return was a compound of surreptitious amusement, overlaid by sly innocence.

'Good morning, Ma'am,' Matty's voice was full of a judicious consideration. 'You're feeling better, I hope?'

Linnet raised her head, met twinkling brown eyes, choked back an answering smile and was grave. 'Much better thank you. I hope I didn't give you too much trouble?' Piers had stage managed this performance of Matty's—she could almost feel his amusement at the way she had picked up her cue and was playing her part. 'It came on so suddenly,' she added vaguely.

'Sudden's the word,' Linnet watched the old housekeeper's eyes slide to meet Piers, 'but no trouble at all.' The dish placed to her satisfaction, the housekeeper straightened and went back to the kitchen.

Through all this, Sheena had remained silent, her face utterly expressionless except for her eyes which glittered like iceberg chips, but as soon as the door closed behind Mrs Matthieson's rotund figure, she attacked.

'That's the worst of these old retainers, Piers. I suppose you've noticed nothing—after all, you see her every day, but I've been away so it's all fresh to me. The woman's positively familiar—speaking to Linnie like that.'

'Why shouldn't she speak to me like that?' Linnet chipped in aggravatingly. 'I've known her for years. In fact, I can remember when Uncle Fergie did a bit of courting in that area. Matty wouldn't have him though, I was there when she sent him off with a flea in his ear.'

'He wasn't the only one,' Piers comforted. 'There were several others, if I remember correctly. Her standard excuse was that they were all too fond of a dram. The late Mr Matthieson never touched a drop!'

This was a digression from Sheena's chosen line of conversation, her lips tightened and she firmly brought the talk back to where she wanted it—the village of Glenardh. In her opinion, it had changed and not for the better. Linnet nibbled at a corner of toast between sips of very hot, black coffee—watching Piers denuding his area of the table of everything edible while he ignored Sheena's comments about deterioration.

'In what way?' Linnet tried to sound interested.

'In every way!' Sheena was sweeping. 'The new hotel, it sticks out like a sore thumb—all those "Bed and Breakfast" signs, nearly every cottage has one. The strangers and the things they're doing to the houses Piers has allowed them to buy—patios, loft conversions—the whole atmosphere of the glen is being ruined. It's not as I knew it when we were children, all the family feeling's gone.'

'If places don't move with the times, they die,' Piers looked up from buttering the last piece of toast. 'And there never was all that much of a family feeling—a village feeling, perhaps, but that's all and I think the new people are fitting in very well—they're certainly improving the look of the place. As for patios, they're a good place to sit in the long summer evenings and in the winter they look a damn sight better than a weed covered patch. I wouldn't mind having one myself only we've no room ...'

'But *selling* cottages ...' Sheena was disapproving.

'I don't,' he was firm. 'Not if there's a young, local couple wanting the place, but if there isn't ...' he shrugged. 'It's better to sell than have them fall into ruins.'

'But it's making everything different,' Sheena mourned and then, appealing to Linnet. 'Don't you think so, Linnie?'

Applied to direct for an opinion, Linnet diplomatically side-stepped the question. 'I don't know,' she murmured. 'Coming back from Creevie, the road doesn't touch the village, it goes round the back of it, but what I've seen from a distance looks very nice and not out of the way. Everything's clean and neat and I saw two new fishing boats.'

'Making an enormous profit taking summer visitors out for the day,' Sheena allowed herself a little moue of distaste. 'Glenardh's become a holiday resort, didn't you know?'

'Which is better than dying,' Piers spared Linnet

the trouble of answering. 'It's no good trying to live in the past, Sheena; it's people who keep villages alive, not hoary old legends. Just remember, the MacArdhs didn't originate here in the glen—we came because we were dispossessed, outlawed and grateful for a place to lay our heads. We were made welcome once and allowed to live peacefully here—surely we can be equally generous?' His grey eyes lighted on Linnet, slid over her, missing nothing of her jeans and sweater—they were even coolly appreciative of the tightness of one and the sloppiness of the other. 'Come along, mo creadh, I've business in the village and you may as well come with me. No,' he stopped her involuntary protest, 'you don't need to change, you'll do very well as you are.'

Linnet scowled at him behind Sheena's back—she'd had no intention of changing! But so far, she'd given the village a wide berth—reluctant to meet old friends for fear of starting a tide of speculation. Not that she'd have known—nobody would be so badly mannered as to ask a question outright, but in the evening, around the firesides, there'd be talk. That sort of thing didn't matter to Piers, he strode through it as though it didn't exist. Maybe, for him, it didn't but she was made of less durable material.

'And I think I may as well come also,' Sheena decided and suddenly Linnet's eyes met her husband's and a smile quivered on her lips. 'Who's chaperoning who?' She mouthed it in a low, husky mutter which went no further than his ears before he had her by the arm and was whisking her through into the hall.

'It'll give them something to clack about,' he murmured as they waited for Sheena and as Linnet slid one arm into her anorak, he shook his head sadly and his hand slid down over her flat stomach. 'Better leave that jacket loose,' he suggested. 'We don't want anybody to think you're hiding something or tongues *will* wag!'

Linnet flushed and dragged the zip right up to the neck. 'As they wagged before?'

'Did they?' He looked down at her flushed face with a leer. 'I didn't hear anything, but then, I wouldn't, would I?'

'You know, I don't think I want to go with you,' she wrinkled her nose in distaste. 'I've only just realised what people must have thought, it never occurred to me they'd think *that* of me.'

'But they probably thought it about me,' he pointed out hardily. 'They'd reason to, if what you say about the previous gossip is true. It *was* a very long deer fence and the sands at Gairloch are beguiling in the moonlight.'

'Which is just the point I was making,' she snapped. '*My* reputation was unsullied until you made a mess of it!'

'Then I'll have to see about making amends,' Piers wasn't taking her seriously and he laughed at her snort of anger.

Glenardh village sheltered at the head of the loch, a straggle of white cottages and houses against the green of low lying pastures and backed by the lower slopes of Beinn Ardh which raised its bald, round head nearly three thousand feet above the water. Linnet scrambled down from the Landrover and looked about her with delight. Piers had parked on the open ground at the lochside just opposite what Sheena had called the 'new' hotel. But it wasn't new, not really—a remake of a couple of the bigger houses which blended in very well, the freshly painted façade offset by the deep green of the shrubs on either side of the entrance.

She remembered the village well—five years wasn't long enough to forget the place where she'd grown up—it had always been neat and clean but now, it had an added shine of prosperity and above it, on the green plateau which was the common land, three sparkling white, touring caravans were parked. In the clear air, she caught the smell of frying bacon and heard, in the distance a clear childish treble calling.

'A few people have discovered Glenardh,' she turned to her husband with a smile and a cocked eyebrow. 'You don't get more?'

'Not so early in the season,' he smiled at her secretively. 'One of the good things about fishermen is that they can keep a secret. They find a good place but they don't broadcast it. The same ones come at this time every year, rain or shine but the place will be full up later in the summer.'

'Tourists!' Sheena sniffed her displeasure and turned her attention to her dog; a small pekinese with bulbous eyes and which looked like a hank of chestnut coloured silk and which, Linnet thought, was going to lose the use of its legs completely if it continued to be carried about.

Piers offered to take her to be introduced to the schoolmaster but she shook her head, leaving him and Sheena to go off to the small school together and once they'd gone, she counted cottages. There was only one person she felt inclined to call on—one in all the glen who wouldn't even *look* a question and she wandered off to knock at an open door which was painted a deep, bright blue.

From within, she heard the clack of a loom and gave a loud cough, a slight clearing of the throat wouldn't have been heard above the noise of the handloom—and was rewarded by a glad cry of 'Linnie! Come your ways in!'

Linnet stepped over the threshold and went back five years in time. Catriona MacDonald was still weaving her tweeds and her old grannie still sat by the fire, near blind eyes looking into space. But it was a warm welcome: a freshly brewed pot of tea, a plateful of assorted scones, a freshly baked bannock and a dish of golden butter. All together with easy conversation where the past wasn't discussed in any personal way and no awkward questions were asked. It was as though she'd never been away, as though she'd called in on her half-day off from the hotel in Creevie as she'd been used to do. Time passed without her realising it and then Piers was stooping his tall head to come under the low lintel.

'Girl talk?' he enquired lazily. 'Where's *my* tea?'

'Just talking over old times,' Catriona threw it over her shoulder as she went off to the dresser for a clean cup. 'Better if we have no men about when we do that.' She came back with the cup and a piece of tweed which she tossed in Linnet's lap. 'Like it? It's my own design. There's a shop in Fort William takes all I can weave—do you think they'll like that one.'

Linnet handled the soft stuff reverently—a mixture of pink and pale mauve which looked like heather blossom. 'If they don't,' she said sturdily, 'you can sell it to me. It's lovely.'

'And enough woven to make a suit for a little thing like you,' Catriona chuckled, 'Grannie said you were coming—she has the sight, you know.'

'Every family has a grannie somewhere who has the "sight",' Piers was derisory. 'They're the bane of Scotland, these "sighted" grannies. Has she "seen" Hamish MacGregor, Cat?'

Catriona tossed her red head while she threw a sparkling glance at Linnet. 'Three years I waited for that man to make up his mind but he was not in a hurry—so now, he must wait for me. Ach! It will take maybe another three years just for me to make up *my* mind!'

'Enjoy your gossip?' The spring sunlight shone bright on Piers' head, turning the mahogany to a deep chestnut as they walked back to the Landrover and at Linnet's nod, 'You see, there was nothing to be afraid of.'

'Hunh!' Linnet looked at him out of the corners of her long blue eyes. 'I wasn't afraid, not of Catriona. *She* never threatened me—*she* was always my friend— which is more than can be said for some,' she added under her breath. 'Where's Sheena?'

'Still closeted with the schoolmaster, arranging the games for May Day.'

'That's early, isn't it?' A little frown wrinkled her forehead as she wrestled with memory. 'I remember it being in August.'

Piers tucked her hand under his arm. 'It's the schoolmaster, he's new, an Oban fellow with strong recollections of the Oban Games which are always held on May Day. But it's not a bad idea, much better than having them in the height of the season when we're crowded out with campers and besides, it's easier on the performers and contestants—think of the pipe bands sweating under their full dress uniform and feather bonnets. Old Jamie Mackie still plays the lament. Sheena doesn't like it though, I've left her and the schoolmaster to fight it out between them,' his mouth curved in a wry grin. 'This is one time when I don't think she'll win. He's a determined young fellow—he'll probably find you something to do as well, I told him you were here.'

'Thank you for nothing,' she assumed hauteur, 'but I'd rather not be included. It's hardly my type of thing besides, I doubt I'll be here.'

'You'll be here,' they'd reached the spot where the Landrover was parked and he stood by it, looking down at her. There was no sign of the famous temper in his face, only a grim determination. 'It will be expected of you,' he added in a chilly tone as though she was behaving like a spoiled child. Linnet's soft mouth tightened and her voice became as chilly as his own.

'Then you'll just have to explain that I rarely do what's expected of me, won't you?'

'Linnet,' his voice was a warning, 'the folk in the glen know you're here so you'll do whatever's necessary as my wife. That's not a request, that's an order. In fact, you'll do any damn thing you're asked; confer with the judges, hand out prizes, pat little children on the head . . .'

'All the things your mother used to do,' she lifted her top lip in a slight sneer. 'I'm hardly fitted for that, am I? Remember, I was a naughty girl—I brought shame on your not so illustrious house. These hands,' she extended them mockingly, 'they're sullied with sin! Hardly suitable for putting wreaths of flowers on little girls' innocent heads!' She looked upwards to see if there was any sign he was relenting, but he looked as implacable as ever. The thick headed idiot! She swore under her breath, ceased to be cool and reasonable and became waspishly sweet with a sting in the tail.

'I gather that Sheena has been taking the leading role in these functions since your mother went off to Edinburgh and it's a part she was practically born for . . .'

'Don't be bitchy,' Piers stopped her before she could really get going. 'We all do our share and if you're worrying about putting wreaths of flowers on tiny heads, I don't suppose they'll wilt if you handle them lightly.'

'And this is your "couple of days"?' She eyed him angrily. 'Now you're getting me involved right up till May Day and that's more than a fortnight away. Surely Sheena's not staying till then?'

'No,' he shook his head at her. 'She'll be gone by the end of the week I hope, but she'll be back so you can look forward to playing your part for quite a while.'

'Not me,' she snapped. 'I'll leave that to Sheena. There's also the matter of my not speaking Gaelic; people will decide you had appalling taste when it came to getting yourself a wife so I shall go back to Blackpool before I shame you again.'

Piers opened his mouth to retort and swiftly closed it again on a curse as Sheena, battle light shining in her eyes came swiftly towards them, the schoolmaster had evidently won this first round but there would be others to come. Linnet schooled her face to an expression of humble admiration and held the pekinese while Sheena climbed into the middle of the front bench seat, after which, she scrambled in herself and was rewarded with a run down of the most recent developments.

'The man's a fool,' Sheena was scornful. 'I told him his plans were too ambitious—we don't want that sort of thing here—we all know where it will lead,' and in case Linnet didn't know, Sheena enlightened her. 'There'll be busloads of people coming and the glen will be a shambles with beer bottles and cans scattered everywhere. We'll have trashy stalls selling rubbish—not the sort of thing we want at all!'

Which concluded the matter, as far as Sheena was concerned and Linnet decided to follow Piers' example and keep a low profile. Personally, she didn't agree. People here lived very quiet lives, they should be allowed the chance once in a while to let everything rip. They took their enjoyments seriously, making the most of them—they *liked* competitions, dancing, pipe music and the strenuous activity of the games and if they made a bit of a mess and some of the men had too much to drink—so what? She shrugged to herself, it had nothing to do with her and she tickled the pekinese behind its long, silky ears to avoid burying her fingers in Sheena's immaculate hairdo and spoiling the carefully ordered, silvery fair waves and curls.

Linnet slunk into dinner that evening in a day length cotton dress which Sheena eyed distastefully. Linnet flushed slightly—it was the best she could manage under the circumstances since Piers had ruined the pink silk and in any case, she hadn't brought anything long with her—nothing comparable with Sheena's flowing silk in a shade of blue which gave a little more colour to her eyes.

'Dinner not ready yet?' Sheena made it sound like a crime. 'Piers, darling,' she raised her voice, 'this house is going to the dogs. It's high time you had somebody here to run it properly.'

Determined to keep clear of family quarrels, Linnet heard herself making an excuse to escape for a while. She'd forgotten her hankie, but Piers was close behind her when she reached the stairs.

'That was a silly excuse,' he reproved her, 'I can see the top of it sticking out of your pocket.'

'I'm *not* making excuses,' she hissed at him, taking the offensive. 'And if you'd stop being so damn suspicious, stop following me and start behaving like a normal, well adjusted human being, we might get somewhere.'

Piers kept up his air of good humour, his mouth smiled, but his eyes didn't and the hand which grasped her arm to prevent her from flying upstairs was going to leave bruises. His soft murmur sounded good tempered as well, except for what he said.

'Don't start a brawl in front of visitors, Linnet.'

'I'll start a bloody war if I feel like it!' she muttered back defiantly. 'Heavens, I can't even make a legitimate excuse to leave the room without you follow to see what I'm doing. Did you think I was going to run off with the silver?' The words died in her throat, ending on a mumble as she felt a cold uneasiness prickle at the back of her neck and turning, found Sheena at the dining room door, listening. Piers must have had the same feeling for he put his hand in his pocket, drew out a clean handkerchief and stuffed it in her fingers without raising his head.

'Use that for now, darling,' he purred, eyes daring her to make a scene. 'A bit big but if it'll save you belting up and down the stairs . . .'

The house might be going to the dogs, but the meal Mrs Matthieson produced was excellent—a fresh tasting, thin vegetable soup with golden brown croutons floating on the top, followed by a pineapple bedecked ham which Piers carved neatly and without fuss. Linnet watched the pink slices falling from the bright steel blade in his capable hand—that was the trouble with the man—he could do everything and whatever he did, he did well.

She ate her dinner in silence, listening to Piers and Sheena as they squabbled amicably about the degree of relationship which existed between them—Piers said 'cousins' but his 'cousin' was opting for something a little more tenuous. 'Oh, I don't think you could call it anything more than kissing kin,' Sheena objected and the rest of the meal was taken up with a set of genealogies which made Linnet's head spin as she tried to sort them out. 'But I'll accept "cousin",' Sheena was gracious as she tried to draw Linnet into the conversation. 'I always feel closer to Piers than to anybody else—I suppose it comes of being brought up with him.'

Linnet nodded and forced back a tart reply which struggled on her tongue for utterance. A reply which would have made mention of a very long deer fence, not to mention the sands at Gairloch, both of which would testify to the closeness of the relationship. Instead, she smiled sweetly and pathetically and said how wonderful it must be to have loads of relatives, all with this wonderful family feeling. For herself, she shrugged and allowed her mouth to droop sadly—she'd never known any other family but Uncle Fergie—it made for a solitary life!

From the gleam in Piers' eyes, she suspected she'd overdone it a bit and his softly growled reply confirmed her suspicions.

'Pass back that handkerchief, you've got me crying!' But the growl was for her ears only—it didn't reach to where Sheena was sitting, still quoting examples of close family feeling.

The bedroom was firelit and she slid out of her clothes listlessly, glad of the warmth before she trailed along to the bathroom in one of Piers' overlong dressing gowns and with her nightie over her arm. Stepping out of the shower, she caught sight of herself in the mirror and assessed her image. *Not* beautiful—passable, maybe but beauty had escaped her. She was too short, her hair, though glossy and thick had no curl. Hurriedly, she wrapped the offending image in a bath towel and rubbed herself dry before sliding into her cotton nightie and pattering back to the bedroom where she switched on the bedside lamp.

And there it was, just as she'd suggested! The basket hilt reposing neatly on the pillows like a fretted steel head and nearly four foot of shining, two edged blade lying precisely down the centre of the bed!

CHAPTER SIX

'AND you're going to need it,' Piers jeered at her from the gloom. 'Although I think you were over ambitious when you suggested it. I doubt if you could lift it, never mind get in a good swipe with it. Perhaps you'd better have this,' and he walked easily into the small pool of light cast by the lamp, only pausing to draw the dirk from his stocking.

He offered it to her, hilt first over the back of his hand. 'Not as sharp as that tongue of yours, wife but it would serve to slit my throat if I become importunate. I'm not spending another night on that couch, not if you were the Goodwife of Laggan in person!'

Linnet accepted the dirk between her finger and thumb, lifting it to examine it—a short, slender blade, rather like a misericorde—fitted into a haft of polished black horn with a silver mount and guard. She wrinkled her nose with distaste and opened her fingers so that the small weapon fell to quiver point down in the floorboards where it twanged audibly as it vibrated to and fro.

'The Goodwife of Laggan was a witch,' she said it conversationally. 'I believe she ate travellers when she wasn't sitting at home and being a model of decorum.'

'That's right, my dear,' he tossed his jacket on to the back of a chair and commenced to undo the buttons of his shirt. 'Like you—a model of decorum on the surface. Pick up the dirk, Linnet, although you won't have to use it. I still don't know whether I can stomach Archie Gow's leavings.'

She whitened at the insult and her hands clenched so tightly, the nails bit into her palms, but she managed to walk steadily past him to the dressing-table where she loosened the knot of her hair and picked up her hairbrush. She could see herself in the mirror although she hardly recognised her reflection. It must be the age of the glass which made her look like a corpse—pallid and drowned.

'No? I didn't think you would,' her voice was quite steady and that pleased her. 'Any more than I'd take Sheena Gow's so that leaves us equal, doesn't it? Pick up your dirk yourself and you can hang that damn sword back on the wall where it belongs. You're not in any danger from me!'

With her eyes closed, she counted out one hundred strokes of the hairbrush, put it down and walked past him to the bed, turning her back on him before he had the opportunity to take off any more clothes. She decorously bunched her nightie about her calves as she scrambled up, pushing back the heavy tester curtain and went very still as his voice came from behind her.

'Why did it have to be Archie?' Piers asked the question quietly, 'Or did you have a perverted taste for the rotten ones?'

Linnet kept her eyes closed and her back firmly turned towards him. 'Archie wasn't rotten,' she sighed wearily. 'He was only weak and easily led.'

'Have you seen him since?'

The question was unexpected but it served its purpose, it dispelled her weariness and brought her back to fighting form. With a yell of pure anger, she sprang, bouncing to her feet on the coverlet, seized the claymore and swung it in as wide an arc as she could manage. 'No, I have *not*!' she yelled. 'I've seen nobody—not you, not Sheena, nobody from the glen and certainly not Archie. If I'd had my way, I'd never have set foot within a hundred miles of any of you, or this place.'

The sight of her struggling with the heavy weapon seemed to amuse him, she caught the flash of his teeth as he smiled, 'Then why come here?'

'Because, unlike you, I'm not a free agent,' she snarled it between her teeth as she lowered the blade to rest her aching arms. 'I'm Ruby's dogsbody. She chose this place, not me. *She* sent me up here. If it had been anybody else but her I wouldn't have come, but where Ruby's concerned—she's my friend as well as my employer. She helped me when there was nobody else—when I had nowhere to go and nobody to turn to. When my *husband* threatened me with God knows what. Although,' she admitted grimly, 'if I'd known what a mess I was going to get into, I'd probably have cut my throat . . .'

'So, we're back to Miss Ruby Lee,' he gave a soft chuckle, 'or should I say "Madame Ruby Lee"?' He held out his hand and she pushed the hilt of the claymore into it, watching as his fingers curled round the handle as to the manner born. It gave her time to think.

'You know,' she made it a flat statement.

'About Madame Lee? Mmm,' he nodded, 'but not until this afternoon. I had my agent make a few enquiries about her . . .'

'And why didn't you ask *me*?' she enquired haughtily as she dropped down on the bed and curled her legs under her. 'Oh, I see, you thought she might have dirty fingernails,' she fired up in defence of her employer. 'Or that she's a charlatan? Well, she isn't!'

'I don't think about her at all,' his mouth tightened, 'I was merely curious about your arrival here, thinking it might be another of your ploys . . .'

'. . . So sorry to disappoint you,' she lay back, huddling on to her side and from the pillow, her voice came muffled. 'I don't go in for ploys, I'm simple minded but not so simple I can't see that what you're doing's going to play hell with a divorce. It's going to take ages.'

'That worries you?' Piers thumped himself on to the bed and switched off the lamp. 'The delay?' and when she didn't answer, he chuckled aggravatingly. 'I've not made up my mind about that—not yet.'

Linnet didn't bother to answer. Answering would only prolong this little hell she was living in. She lay awake in the darkness, curled up into the smallest possible space for fear of touching or being touched by him—and aching with the want of him.

This was as it should be, as it had to be—she'd made her vow and she would keep it. Piers would have to accept her as she was, if he wanted her—he'd either have to tell her he didn't believe Archie's story, or better still, that he didn't care and as she didn't have much hope of him saying either of those things, the future looked very dim. She found herself choking on hysterical laughter at the romantic farce they were playing. A man and his wife, together in bed and with a memory keeping them apart—he shouldn't have bothered with the claymore, he should have brought that damn painting down and put it between them—

she gulped back on tears. If it wasn't so bloody funny, she'd cry her eyes out!

Linnet woke to the soft, pale light of early morning, instantly aware of where she was and what had happened, which was precisely nothing. Last night she'd thought she'd never sleep, that she'd go mad first, but now the night had passed and it was morning. She'd slept after all and she hadn't gone mad. It was amazing what a difference a bit of daylight made to everything. She felt easier, as though some problem had been solved while she slept—but, of course, nothing had been solved. The only difference was that Piers was still asleep and until he woke, she could let her guard drop.

Moving stealthily, she slid out of bed to tiptoe round to his side and look down at his sleeping face. Her fingers itched to push back the lock of hair which had fallen over his high forehead, but she controlled the desire and tried to study him as though he was a stranger and this was the first time she'd seen him.

The early light took all the colour out of things so that, against the whiteness of the pillows and sheets, his hair looked almost black. 'Some say he's black but I say he's bonny,' the words of the old song trickled through her mind. 'My handsome, winsome Johnny.' Softly, she turned away and he spoke before she'd taken a step.

'Ach, but you're the uncomfortable woman to have in a bed. Where are you off to now?'

'Wash, dress and a nice walk before breakfast,' she was curt, intending to get out of the room as soon as possible, but something held her back and she knew what that something was. All the time she'd been away from him, she'd felt as though she was bleeding to death—seeing him asleep, unconscious of her presence, had been like a soothing balm. If only he'd have the normal muzzy period of adjustment between sleeping and waking, instead of being one thing or the other.

'Tonight,' he said it with relish, 'tonight, I have the dirk. You were snoring a bit and when I put my hand over your mouth to stop you, you bit my finger!'

'Mmm,' she manufactured a satisfied grin—things *were* easier, 'I'm a vampire by nature, I hope I drew blood. You'd better mind I don't go for your neck next time, you'd wake up all pale and listless.'

'There are other ways of making me wake pale and listless,' he reminded her with an innocent smile and her mouth curved into a wry grimace.

'Shame on you, sir!' It sounded very brave, almost careless and she was pleased with herself. 'Is this the man who wouldn't soil his hands with another man's leavings?'

'At night, all cats are grey; in the dark, I could pretend you were another cat,' his hand came to clutch at a fold of her nightie. 'A stranger cat, one I've never met before.'

'Piers,' she made it as stern as possible. 'I'm here because you insisted on it, because you made it impossible for me to refuse your—er—hospitality. I'm not here of my own free will. You said I had to behave myself—do as I was told—which I'm doing—and in return, you'd leave me alone. A bargain's a bargain and I'm keeping my side of it, but that doesn't seem to be good enough for you. You promised me this bed to myself, but I should have known better than to trust you. Tonight, *you* can have the bed, the claymore, the dirk, the lot because I'm having the couch.'

'Scared?'

'Certainly not,' she tilted her chin defiantly. 'I just won't be used.' Slowly, finger by finger, she prised his hand away from the folds of her nightie, scolding as she did so. 'You've already ruined my best pink silk and my bath wrap, I'll be damned if I let you tear my nightie to bits!' And free at last, she stalked off to the bathroom with clean jeans and a tee shirt over her arm and her hand full of underwear.

When she returned, neat and glowing from a cold shower, he was sitting on the side of his bed in his dressing gown. 'Wait for me,' he suggested. 'It's early yet; we'll have a cup of tea before we go.'

'*We?*' She raised her nose snootily, 'I don't recall inviting *you!*'

'No, you didn't,' he made it agreeable. 'But I'm not suggesting anything improper so don't look like that, as though there's a bad smell under your nose. Where d'you fancy walking?'

'Along the lochside,' she was prompt. 'Maybe even as far as Glenardh. I'm saving the hills for later, they look different with all those new spruce and fir plantations. I wish the Forestry people would try for a little more variety. Shall you be long?'

'Ten minutes,' he rasped his hand over his chin and grimaced. 'I think I'll grow a beard.'

'Ugh!' she gave a dramatic shudder. 'Pardon me if I don't watch. I've always hated hairy men.'

'But you didn't mind Archie's . . .'

'Pooh!' Linnet was on the way to the door and she threw the words over her shoulder. 'That wispy thing he wore—it was only something for the poor laddie to hide behind. I'll go and make the tea while I'm waiting.'

Poor Archie—her thoughts ran on as she plugged in the kettle and set out crockery; Archie, who was a paler, younger edition of Sheena, his sister, without an ounce of her forcefulness or her strength of will. Nothing would ever make him a he-man, not even a wispy set of silvery whiskers. They'd only ever accentuated his weak chin, but try as she would, she'd never been able to dislike him, not as she disliked his sister. It was no wonder their father had left his money and his chain of supermarkets to his strong minded daughter. Archie would have lost the lot in a few months.

It was good to walk first thing in the morning, the sun wasn't yet high enough to have dried up the night's dew and everything was fresh and sparkling. The loch glittered with myriad points of reflected light, little waves creamed along the edges of it, stirring the clumps of seaweed on the rocks and ruffling the surface until it sparkled. Above the dark, round topped pines which rimmed the loch, the summit of Beinn Ardh was still clothed in its shroud of morning mist and Linnet sniffed with pleasure before the gloom settled on her once more so that, although she stepped out briskly, there was little joy in her and she didn't speak.

'What's the matter?' Piers broke the silence which had lasted all the way to the village and halfway back. 'You disappoint me, Linnet—you're not usually so short of words.'

'Ach,' she mimicked Catriona. 'I was just thinking. I like to devote a part of *every* day to thought.'

'And what was your thought for the day?'

'How much longer you're going to make me play this farce,' swiftly, she reverted to her normal speech, the lilt leaving her voice and the words coming out flat and uncompromising. 'We can't keep this up for ever,' she pointed out. 'Leave out the wider implications and concentrating just on the two of us—if we were ordinary friends, it wouldn't be so bad but there's no friendship between us. We just tear each other to pieces—we'll probably end up trying to murder each other,' she added darkly—walking on a few paces before stopping dead in her tracks and turning to face him. 'I'm not going to ask how you intend to explain away this little interlude because I know you won't bother with anything as mundane as an explanation,' gradually, she became sarcastic, 'that would be far too simple. Everybody has got to accept that after an absence of five years, I've popped up again like the bad fairy and I'm welcomed back at Eilean Ardh as though I'd only been away for a weekend.'

'I don't see the need to explain anything,' Piers looked tranquilly out over the water. 'What we do is *our* business . . .'

'*Your* business,' she corrected. 'But you've involved me in it and that, I don't like, so I'm going back to the lodge after breakfast and you can do and say what you like. The deal's off!'

'No,' his eyes were still tranquil when he looked back at her chilly little face. 'My wife stays in *my* house . . .'

'. . . even if you don't want her any more,' she interrupted bitterly. 'I know all that, you've said it before. You sound more like a dog in a manger every minute—your pride's a running sore and you'd rather pick it, make it worse than let it get better. I'm not built that way. I want all this concluded, one way or the other, *now*!'

'I'm working on it,' he shrugged. 'Who knows—with a little adjustment on both sides, we could possibly salvage something . . .'

'And be condescended to for the rest of my life? Not likely!' She was fierce. 'I see you, hear you and it stirs up memories . . .'

'Nice ones?'

'No, you self-righteous bastard—only insults and threats. I won't, I can't live with that!'

'And all this because I shared your bed last night . . .'

'You and a load of ironmongery,' she was swift to break in—the argument was stimulating and her gloom lifted. 'You can fill that bed up with whatever you like—a couple of pikes and a battleaxe for all I care—you're not having me in it!'

Piers' eyebrows lifted and his lips twitched in an effort not to smile. 'I was thinking more along the lines of a scold's bridle,' he murmured softly and there was a glint in his eyes which should have warned her, but she was in no mood to pay attention to it.

'Go the whole hog,' she snapped. 'A flintlock pistol, a set of chain mail . . .'

'. . . and a chastity belt,' he added for good measure. 'I think we've got one of those somewhere, but you wouldn't sleep comfortably in it. Last night, while you were snoring like a little pig, I had plenty of time to think, about us and about the future—so get this straight—I'm not divorcing you and I'm going to make sure you don't divorce me . . .'

'But if I leave personalities out of it,' her spurt of temper died as she had a vision of the future—a hopeless, grey area, devoid of love and understanding—she felt flat and desperate. 'Incompatibility, that should do it or you could take a girl friend for a randy night at an hotel—I'm sorry, I don't know the drill for these things, I haven't gone into it. Or you could divorce me, you've grounds—desertion—one of us could set up house with somebody . . .'

'You'd do that?' It was a swift question and it caught her unawares so that she answered without thinking.

'No, I damn well wouldn't,' as she spat it out, she realised her mistake and her temper rose while inside, she wept. Piers had always had this ability to make her uncertain so that she oscillated between rage and despair—she couldn't control her emotions any longer. She stepped back from the open road, backing up against the pale trunk of a young birch which had taken root at the side of the ditch—and shuddered away from the menace in his face. 'Leave me alone,' she muttered, almost hysterically with an unknown fear thick on her tongue. 'I don't want . . .'

'But you do, my dear, sexy little wife,' it was almost a whisper as he followed to put a hand on either side of her, pinning her to the slender trunk. 'You always did! I knew that before we were married and I was easy on you—not a touch the whole village couldn't have seen because you were young and I didn't think you could handle it. But Archie'd been there before me, hadn't he? No wonder you ran away when it came my turn.'

'You lousy, rotten . . .' she swung at him but he caught her wrist before her hand could connect and jerked her into his arms.

'Was it like this, Linnet?' as he pulled her close and

found her mouth with his own. 'Tell me,' it was a furious mutter against her lips, 'was it as good as this?'

His hands slid under her tee shirt, she felt them fumble with the catch of her bra and his fingers closed cruelly as her breasts spilled out into his hands. He was leaning heavily against her and the slender birch trunk was pressing viciously into her spine, but then, the pressure of his mouth slackened and what had been savage and uncaring of hurting her was warm and seductive, turning her limbs to water.

'Hell!' She heard his mutter in a hazy dream. 'I still want you, you termagant.' The hands at her breast were no longer punishing, not hurting any more but caressing seductively and she felt the thrust of his hips against her.

But it wasn't love! Amid the wild beat of her heart and the thunder of the blood in her veins; the little cold thought trickled into a dark, chilly chamber of her mind to grow and send its tendrils right through her—killing her involuntary response so that she could remain still and remote as if all this was happening to somebody else and she was only a bystander.

'A highlander is nearly impossible to civilise,' she quoted from a book in a cold, remote way. 'Whatever you do, he remains a savage in a kilt. You *did* say "in the straw", didn't you Piers? Only in the straw. Does a dry ditch come under that heading?' From somewhere, she found courage and raised her eyes to his without anything in them but a harsh contempt. 'There's a ditch just behind me and I daresay it would do. Not quite deep enough, we'd be visible from the road if anybody passes but that shouldn't worry *you*. It's not as if you were making love to your wife—only teaching her a lesson in priorities.'

He eased his weight from her and took a pace backwards. 'That's something I should have done when you were eighteen,' all the passion was gone and he was wry now and as cool as she. 'Come on, let's go back and have breakfast.'

'No,' as he grew cool, she felt herself heating up. She shook her head violently and her soft mouth hardened into a firm line. 'I don't go back to that house with you—not now—not ever!'

'Don't make promises you can't keep,' he advised. 'You'll come back to the house and you'll look as though you're enjoying it—because, in a perverted way, you are. I think you like sailing too close to the wind and walking on the edges of precipices. So, tread very carefully, my sweet—one little slip and I'll be waiting to catch you.'

'To beat me?' And she flinched away as his hands slid once more under her tee shirt but he gave her a little shake.

'I'm only putting you back in order, mo creadh,' his fingers found the catch of her bra and fastened it. 'We don't want anybody to think we can't control our lust for each other.'

Linnet sensed the actual danger was over, at least for the time being and she snorted softly. 'You don't care what anybody thinks.' She flushed slightly as he brushed some scraps of papery bark from the seat of her jeans and out of her hair, undoing her ponytail in the process so that her hair fell about her shoulders in black, silky strands.

'Not much,' and as if nothing had happened

between them, he gave her a swift grin. 'But I have to think of you and what Sheena might deduce if I took you back looking tumbled. Who knows, you might even remember how to blush.'

'And Ruby?' she reminded him. 'She pays me, you know—she's depending on me . . .'

'A bridge we'll cross when we come to it,' he grasped her arm and held it firmly as they walked back to Eilean Ardh.

Linnet disdained a reply, contenting herself with a lethal glance which had no effect—he didn't appear to notice it or, if he did, it bounced off his armour and she felt discouraged. Fate was against her, but she perked up when she thought of how well she'd coped so far. She'd taken the appalling and disastrous coincidence of Ruby choosing this place in her stride, had'nt she and in May, when Ruby arrived—but May was a fortnight away.

Never mind, nothing much could happen in a fortnight—it was a comforting thought and she hugged it to herself. Nothing could happen if she didn't want it to and she didn't—she didn't! And he wouldn't get all his own way with Ruby—that was one lady he couldn't cozen. Ruby paid generously, but she expected value for money so there'd be plenty to do and with all that, she, Linnet would be able to blend into the background unobtrusively—leave Piers to work out his own destiny and cope with the awkwardness. In fact, her mouth took on a sardonic curve, he would have to cope with everything—she would be remote and disinterested; it would be safer that way.

'I'll ask you for the second time,' Piers' voice at last penetrated and she gave a little start at the friendliness

of it. 'I'm going fishing after breakfast—d'you want to
come with me?'

'Sorry, I was miles away,' she waved her hand
airily. 'No thank you, I told you, I'm going back to the
lodge.'

The friendliness vanished. 'No, Linnet. You haven't
been listening. We, you and I are on a salvage
operation—we haven't much, but we're going to find
out if it's enough.'

'You've changed your tune.'

'With reason, mo creadh.' He turned her to face him
and there was no cruelty in his hands. 'What we had,
part of it is still there after five years. It's only the
physical side, I admit, but it hasn't died for either of
us, has it. You still want me and I still want you so
we'll make that do until we grow together or . . .' He
gave her a mocking grin, 'Starvation doesn't seem to
have killed it, so that's not the remedy . . .'

'You mean we should put it on the menu, working
on the "overkill" principle?' It was costing her a lot to
just stand there, talking like this, as though they were
discussing trying out a remedy on rabbits or
guinea-pigs. 'I don't think I'm ready for anything like
that—besides, as I said, there's Ruby or would you
spare me to her during the daylight hours?'

'And as I said,' he gave her a little shake, 'we've
nearly a fortnight before your Ruby arrives and I'm
not going to rush things. We ought to give ourselves a
few days of merely being friendly—see how we get on.
That's why I suggested the fishing today and there's
no need for you to be afraid. I could hardly rape you
offshore, in a boat.'

'And the alternative?'

'Linnet,' it came as an exasperated growl, 'you've three options—you can go with Sheena and harry the schoolmaster—poor devil, I'd not be in his shoes for all the tea in China—not with the two of you on his back—or you can retire to the bedroom in one of your sulks or, you can come with me in the boat and bait the hooks.'

Linnet speculated silently on the other alternative which involved waiting until he'd left in the boat and then somehow getting herself and her cases across to the lodge. No difficulty there, Sheena would be only too glad to oblige with a lift. Then get into her car and drive like hell, away from this place—but she decided against this, she didn't think it would do any good. She'd run away once before and it hadn't worked; a malevolent Fate had stepped in and thrown her back into the melting pot.

It was like playing snakes and ladders: you hopped along, climbed ahead and then a throw of the dice landed you on the wrong square and you slid back to where you'd started. Life was a vicious circle and Linnet found herself wishing Piers had let her drown in the loch!

'I'll fish,' but she said it reluctantly and without enthusiasm.

Sheena didn't like the idea, her pale eyes sparkled with fury but her calm face registered only a passing and very slight disapproval. 'I was counting on your support against the May Day scheme, Linnet.'

'It's not my scene,' Linnet regretted the words as soon as she'd said them, as soon as she'd caught Piers' warning look. Now Sheena would let it be known far and wide that Piers' wife wasn't interested in village happenings. She shrugged it off. Whatever she did was going to be wrong so she'd better grow a thick skin and learn to live with her mistakes.

The boat was the same one into which Piers had hauled her from the loch and Linnet passed the foodbasket down to him before she jumped from the jetty to land lightly beside him.

'Oh lord,' she groaned as she caught sight of the waiting bucket of dead fish and the sharp knife lying beside it. 'This takes me back years! I always had the skivvy's job, the one nobody else wanted—chopping off strips of bait and skewering them and myself on the hooks. What are you going after?'

'Haddock, whiting, mullet, anything we can catch,' he shouted it and the wind whipped the words from his mouth. 'Matty's always glad of fresh fish and this morning, Catriona mentioned she could do with some as well.'

Linnet made a disgusted sound at the back of her throat, 'And them with two new fishing boats . . .'

'Strictly commercial,' he pointed out gravely. 'The catches are sold as soon as they're landed at Ullapool.' Piers jerked his head at the bait bucket and the trolling line with its rows of hooks. 'Get busy, Linnet while I take us outside.'

'Outside, that sounds wonderful, we'll be able to see the Ísles properly. I've always loved islands,' Linnet's fingers, unaccustomed to handling slippery fish, shook a little as she wielded the knife. 'Did your grandmother not come from Mull?'

'Mmm, a MacLean and didn't she rub it in,' he chuckled. 'Remember the tale about the MacLeans?'

'How they're supposed to be the oldest clan in the world?' Linnet giggled and lapsed into the soft, lilting speech of the Highlands. 'Ach! There were no MacLeans on the Ark—they *already* had a boat of their own!' She paused thoughtfully, the knife poised for cutting but her eyes on the dim shapes of the Isles which seemed to be floating in the sea. 'Isn't it odd how Highlanders all seem to have this long memory— remembering things which happened hundreds of years ago and talking about them as though they took place yesterday or last week.'

'Typically Celtic,' Piers had got through the narrow entrance and was now on a north westerly course. 'The long nights had something to do with it—nothing to do but sit around the fire and tell stories.'

'And hark back over old wrongs, bear grudges,' Linnet raised her head from the bait bucket and looked at him squarely. 'That just about sums you up, doesn't it? Old grievances—too long remembered!'

She worked in silence after that—she had no need to ask where the MacArdhs were from—that, she knew. They were a tiny sept of the MacGregors and when that clan had been outlawed, dispossessed, disarmed and the name forbidden, the MacArdhs had migrated north from their homeland near Loch Lomond and eventually settled here in the glen. She stole a glance at Piers—yes, he'd pass very well for a red MacGregor—proud as the devil and never admitting he was beaten. Courage or sheer pigheadedness? Sometimes, she thought there wasn't much difference between the two. Piers would always do what *he* thought to be right and be damned to the consequences or anybody else's opinion.

Her eyes misted with tenderness and she swiftly transferred her gaze back to the bait bucket.

CHAPTER SEVEN

IT was nearly seven in the evening before Piers
dropped Linnet and a small portion of the catch off at
the stone jetty of Eilean Ardh, before he went on with
the remaining fish to the village landing stage. It had
been a good, pleasant afternoon despite her initial
fears and now, she was pleasantly tired, extremely
hungry and—she looked down at jeans covered with
fish scales and stained with salt water—not fit to be
seen or smelled. With her foot on the bottom tread of
the staircase and her mind unable to think of anything
but a hot bath and a change of clothes before dinner,
Sheena's cool, commanding voice halted her.

'Linnie,' Sheena stood well back as though she
might be contaminated. 'I'd like to have a word with
you.'

'Like this?' Linnet waved a hand which encompassed
her filthy jeans. 'Won't you give me a chance to
change? You sound rather serious and you can hardly
expect me to hold my end up when I look and smell
like this.'

'My dear girl,' Sheena drawled indifferently,
although Linnet noticed she kept her distance. 'What
do you mean? Keep your end up? Do you suppose I
intend to brawl with you?'

'No,' Linnet admitted. 'You and brawling hardly go
together. Very well, if you insist—but,' as Sheena
started to head away in the direction of the breakfast

parlour, 'you can say what you have to say here and please make it as short as possible. Fire away,' and her hand tightened on the banister rail as she leaned against it for support. 'I'm listening.'

The older woman made no bones about it. 'When are you leaving?'

'Leaving?' Linnet temporised while she watched her knuckles grow white against the tan of her hand.

'Yes, leaving,' standing as Linnet was on one stair, Sheena's icy eyes were on a level with her own. 'Leaving Glenardh, but if that's too precipitate— leaving this house. That would do for the present.'

Linnet shrugged, mustering up all the *savoir-faire* at her command, which wasn't much. 'Unlike you,' she said quietly, 'I can't walk out of the glen just when I wish and as for leaving this house, I think that's something you should take up with Piers. I'm here at his request.' She could have said 'command' but she didn't think it wise.

Sheena made a small, angry sound as though she was fast losing her patience. 'My dear girl, I hesitate to say this but—your presence here is just the tiniest bit embarrassing. I don't think you realise . . .'

'I realise a lot,' Linnet snapped back quickly. 'More perhaps than you give me credit for, but as I said, I'm not a free agent. Talk to Piers if you wish but don't try to bully me.'

'You are being deliberately obstructive,' Sheena's beautifully shaped mouth thinned with temper. 'I know what you're trying to do, but you won't get away with it. Piers will never accept what happened between you and Archie . . .'

Linnet broke in with a hoot of mocking laughter.

'What happened between me and Archie! Come on, Sheena, who d'you think you're kidding? You know as well as I do what happened, precisely nothing—I don't know how you talked Archie into that miserable little "confession"—money, I suppose—you've always held the purse strings ever since your father died . . .' Her very blue eyes widened with wonder as she watched Sheena regain her superb self control. The lovely mouth softened from a hard line and the perfect oval of the face became cool and composed while the tall, stately figure lost all signs of tenseness.

'I've packed for you,' Sheena said it gently, 'everything's ready and I'll drive you round to the lodge myself. I'm doing what I think is best for everybody . . .'

'Best for you, you mean,' Linnet snorted her disgust and turned to run up the stairs, but Sheena's slender, graceful hand closed on her arm with surprising strength.

'Will you go!' Sheena kept her grip on Linnet's arm but her manner became placatory. 'Linnie, I'm only trying to save you, save us all a lot of embarrassment. Archie's arriving this evening, in time for dinner and I'm hoping he'll stay a few days. You know it will be difficult and I do like things to run smoothly. I wish I could have given you more time but he rang me from Inverary only just after you and Piers left on your fishing trip . . .'

'Archie's coming here doesn't worry me,' Linnet interrupted.

'But it worries me,' Sheena's hand tightened further and Linnet winced at the hardness of the grip. 'Archie . . .'

'What's that?' Piers had come in silently from the back entrance and was standing in the dimness at the back of the hall. 'Sheena, did you say Archie was coming? Here?'

'This was his home, Piers and the poor darling's been ill,' Sheena soothed. 'He's quite worn out and I thought, under the circumstances you wouldn't mind. Isn't it better this way—the old scandal forgotten and forgiven—everything back to normal, as it used to be . . .' she made a little moue of distress at Piers' disgusted expression. 'You weren't here, my dear, so I couldn't ask you. I simply followed the rules of Highland hospitality. We can hardly turn him away . . .'

'*We?* I can!' Piers came to stand beside Linnet, his arm an iron band about her waist.

'But he's your cousin,' Sheena's iron control slipped and her nicely modulated voice became a trifle shrill. 'What will people think? He comes to see *me* and you forbid him the house . . .'

'Sometimes, you amaze me,' Piers was sarcastic. 'Especially about relationships. Only last evening you were stressing how very distant was the link between us but now, suddenly, Archie's a full cousin. He's no such thing—kin, maybe but a cousin, no!'

'We've room to spare,' Sheena's mouth became obstinate.

'*We?* Again, my dear, you've got it all wrong.' Piers wasn't being obstinate, merely implacable. '*I've* no room under my roof for your brother. Not only do I not want him in the house, I don't want him in the glen either. He's an embarrassment so, meet him outside when he arrives and get rid of him.'

'But what will people say?' Sheena had tears in her eyes and Linnet was undecided whether they were caused by grief or fury. 'At least, let him have a meal before he starts back . . .'

'He can eat mine,' Piers gave way on a minor point, but otherwise, he was as hard and unyielding as a rock. 'I'll take Linnet into Creevie for dinner while you see he's gone by the time we return. If he isn't, I'll throw him in the loch!' And with his arm still about her, Piers swept Linnet upstairs to the bedroom, almost carrying her.

She was breathing hard when he stood her on her feet and carefully closed the door—her eyes drifted about, first to the wall over the fireplace where she could see the claymore had joined its mate. 'Thanks for replacing the hardware,' she murmured.

'And what's this?' His eyes lighted on the suitcases, standing ready packed. 'As soon as my back's turned . . .' This was accompanied by a savage kick at the nearest.

'Here we go again,' she said it resignedly as she stooped to pick up several items which had fallen out when the suitcase turned turtle. 'Threats, threats and more threats. No, don't!' as he grabbed handfuls of things and commenced cramming them into the drawers of a chest. 'You'll get them all crumpled. Damn you, Piers, will you stop behaving like a savage,' she stole a sideways look at him. 'You're not doing any good, you know.'

'What are you pawing through those cases for? And,' he stopped and looked at her closely. 'What d'you mean, I'm not doing any good?

Linnet dealt with the first part first. 'I'm looking for

something not too crumpled to wear to dinner tonight, of course! Drat you, I haven't anything but that cotton dress since you ruined my best pink silk. I shan't forgive you for that easily, I was very fond of it and it was practically new . . .'

'. . . And?' He eyed her balefully.

'And you're not doing any good forbidding Archie the house,' she was cross as she smoothed out a bundle of smalls he'd crammed in a drawer. 'Or when you threatened to throw him in the loch—not, that is if you really mean it about taking me out to dinner. By the time we get back, Archie will be as drunk as a wheelbarrow—he won't be in any condition to drive his car so he'll have to stay.'

'And I'm supposed to smile and entertain my wife's seducer?'

By this time, Linnet had herself well in hand. 'Did he?' she enquired wearily—'Oh, I see. He *must* have done because he said so and you believed him. What a mad, mad world we live in!' And, selecting a few garments, she stalked out of the room, bristling with repressed anger and with her head held very high.

Bathing took a long time. She scrubbed and scrubbed until she was sure she no longer smelled of fish and she washed and rinsed her hair twice—singing loudly all through her ablutions as though she hadn't a care in the world and when she finally returned to the bedroom, it was to find Piers, cool, calm and collected, with not a trace of temper showing, sitting on the edge of the bed and sifting through the contents of one of her cases. The anger was still in him but he was controlling it beautifully.

'You sound happy,' he accused and proffered a

patchwork cotton skirt, very full, in pinks and blues and a crocheted top in gold coloured thread which pretended to be silk. 'Why can't you wear these?'

Linnet gave them a cursory glance. 'I could—they'll make me look about sixteen, but they're as old as the hills so it won't matter if I get them spoiled when I have to jump into the loch to fish Archie out, will it?'

'If Archie goes into the loch,' Piers seemed quite taken by the idea, 'You won't be doing any jumping in to rescue him. We'll let him drown! I didn't know he drank that much.'

'No,' she was silky. 'You were too busy inspecting deer fences and getting yourself stranded at Gairloch to observe anything else. Archie's an alcoholic—I think your mother tried to control him but if he's been away by himself . . .'

'You think he'll be in a bad state?'

Linnet nodded emphatically. 'I'll put money on it.'

Piers reached into the back pocket of his jeans, all his temper gone and his eyes gleaming with a reckless light. Any kind of wager appealed to the Celt in him. 'How much?'

'We-ell,' a reluctant smile curved her mouth. 'It's getting on for the end of the month so I haven't a lot to spare—make it a fiver.'

From his wallet, he extracted a crumpled note and laid it on the dressing table. 'Cover it,' he ordered and Linnet searched in her bag for her purse and laid another note on top of his.

'But you'll lose, you know,' she shook her head mockingly. 'Two large whiskies and Archie's very cheerful—four or five and he's on top of the world—

after that, he's comatose. Make it a tenner,' she challenged him. 'I'm on to a sure thing!'

'I can't afford to lose that much,' suddenly he stooped his head and his mouth found hers. Neither savage nor angry but warm, sweet and very satisfying so that behind her closed lids, her eyes swam with tears and she found herself clinging to him, prolonging the kiss and feeling deprived when he raised his head. 'If you'd settle for a sandwich at the bar and an early night,' the whisper came seductively in her ear, 'I could maybe spare another pound.'

Common sense reasserted itself and she pulled herself free of him—he was behaving as he had five years ago—the same, almost sly humour, the same tenderness and it nearly broke her heart. 'No, it'd be a shame to take your money—besides,' she heard herself sounding practical, 'we only had sandwiches on the boat and I'm starving.' She sniffed and wrinkled her nose. 'Ugh! You smell of fish, hadn't you better bathe and change? You'd better or we *will* be sitting in the bar—that's if they let us in the place at all.'

But when he'd gone off to the bathroom, her face dropped in lines of sadness. Oh, she *knew* she could make him happy, given the chance. She *knew* they could salvage every last little thing, but wanting wasn't enough. He had to love her—love her and prove it by trusting her. She wouldn't commit herself for anything less than that.

Archie wasn't quite as drunk as a wheelbarrow when Linnet and Piers returned from dinner at the Creevie hotel. He was conscious, if not very coherent, but when he tried to rise to his feet, he appeared to need three legs to stand on so he flopped back on to the couch and didn't try to rise again. He leered at Linnet owlishly while his sister made excuses for him. He hadn't been well—he'd picked up a bug in Florence or Venice—he'd driven too far, he was overtired. The best thing for him was bed.

'In the loch,' Piers was being devilish and Sheena's eyes hardened with exasperation as he continued with relish, 'I'll be kind, I'll drop him in the Otter where he can't drown.'

Linnet, who'd cured her nervousness by drinking a couple of glasses of wine with her dinner of spiced lamb chops, sautéd potatoes and a side salad, giggled. The Otter had nothing to do with the gay little, aquatic mammal of that name—it was a corruption of the Gaelic 'oitir' meaning a ford or shallow place and it lay between Eilean Ardh and the lochside, very close to the bridge. It wasn't fordable nowadays, not unless one was on horseback and then, only at low tide.

'He'll sink like a stone,' she protested. 'It's nearly high tide. Leave him where he is until morning, Piers.'

Archie rewarded her with a stupid grin and a mumbled 'thanks' and she looked at him clinically. How had anybody ever made Piers imagine she'd preferred this weedy, colourless man to him? Archie was a drunk, a gambler and as weak as water—there was no substance to him. Piers followed the direction of her gaze with hard, unforgiving eyes.

'You've a kind heart,' he answered her formally. 'Till tomorrow, it is, but,' he marched across to the sideboard and turned the key which locked down the arms of the old fashioned tantalus. 'He's having no more of my whisky. Throw a rug over him, Sheena and I'll have him swept out in the morning.'

Disdaining Archie's inebriated giggle and Sheena's thin, angry protest, Piers swept Linnet out of the sitting room and up the stairs. Once in the bedroom, he solemnly handed her the two five pound notes from the dressing table.

'They're yours,' he gave a deep sigh of regret. 'You won them fair and square, but remind me not to bet with you again. I was relying, depending on Sheena being able to keep him in order.'

You would. But she didn't say it aloud. She turned her back on him while the cog wheels of her mind spun ever faster until they meshed. This visit of Archie's was no accident—no spur of the moment thing. Sheena must have sent for him as soon as she heard Linnet was back in the glen, probably before she arrived herself. And Archie would obey his sister's summons. The allowance which his father had left him was nowhere near adequate for his expensive tastes so his sister was his paymaster. She only had to wave her cheque book and Archie'd come running.

And allowing him to drink too much—that hadn't been an accident either. Sober, Archie might, just might, revert to his devastating honesty. He was one of those peculiar people who rarely told lies unless he was drunk. Basically, he was weak but honest, the weakness predominating and Linnet had the idea he used alcohol to hide behind because he didn't like the look of himself when he was sober.

Piers broke in on her thoughts. 'Are you going to share the bed with me or not.'

'Not!' She pulled herself together with an effort. Share a bed with him, settle for what he offered? Never! The present arrangement was bad enough, a commitment based on logic and common sense and influenced by Piers' somewhat rigid code of behaviour. There was no logic to love and precious little which was sensible about it. 'The couch will do me,' she forced herself to be airy, 'and if I pull that whacking great footstool up beside it, I shan't roll off in the night.'

'I've offered you a share of the bed,' Piers was bland, 'although I can't promise anything. To be honest, last night was a bit of a strain.'

'And by all means, let's be honest,' she scolded tartly. 'You've just said, although you may not know it, that neither your promises nor your terms and arrangements mean very much. You can change them at will.' She had the idea that it was only the wine she'd drunk which was talking, but it sounded good to her ears. 'As for sharing, no, thank you. I'm fussy about a little thing called motivation and I don't think I'd enjoy the aftermath of being a martyr.'

'But you might enjoy being a martyr,' he held her loosely from behind, a hand on each of her shoulders so that she could see his reflection alongside hers in the mirror as she removed the pink studs from her ears.

'No.' She attempted to step away from him but immediately, his hands tightened and she schooled her face to stillness. 'I don't think I'm ready for that yet. It's too soon and I have to be sure there's something worthwhile to salvage. It's all right for you, you can look at this from a purely masculine point of view but I'm a woman, and for me, it's different.'

'You mean you want the romance, the moonlight, the scent of roses and the usual line in love talk?' He lowered his head until their two faces were on the same level in the mirror and his cheek was touching hers. 'I can provide that as well, Linnet, although not the roses, it's the wrong time of year. Would you settle for a bunch of daffodils?'

Firmly, he turned her to face him, his hands slipping from her shoulders to her waist and drawing her close. He was looking down at her in the old, half tender, half mocking way but the mockery wasn't for her, it was for himself—she knew that. He despised her, yet he wanted her and he despised himself for that wanting. It made her angry.

'Here it comes,' she snarled softly, hiding behind a blasé mask. 'The old routine. Don't you men ever think of something original? Ever since this morning, I've been waiting for something like this, wondering when your good intentions and your high minded principles would slip. "Linnet",' she parodied his deep voice, ' "I want you and you want me. We've something we can salvage. We won't rush it." And I swallowed it! But what does it come down to when you reach rock bottom, I'll tell you! There's a woman conveniently to hand and you haven't been on the tiles for a while so all your fine words get lost. Now, it's "Linnet, share my bed" and I think you honestly believe I'll change my mind!' Her blasé mask had slipped and she was working herself up into a fine old rage—the words dripped from her tongue like vitriol. She hurt so much, her only relief was in hurting back.

'I could make you change your mind,' he pulled her more closely against him, arrogantly waiting for the response which her body was too weak to hide and when it came, he gave her a triumphant smile. 'Now, this minute and you can't deny it.'

'Did I ever?' She went on whipping up her rage. 'I didn't deny it when I was eighteen, but you had a little more consideration for me then. But of course, that was a different kettle of fish, wasn't it? You had some respect for me. It wasn't just wanting, you said—it was love! We could wait, you said. We had all our lives in front of us, you said—and love would last forever, *you said*! Ha! Forever was only until you saw that damn painting. You go on up to your bloody Room and make love to *that*! Take *it* a bunch of daffodils!'

'*It* wouldn't appreciate them,' he stooped his tall head and nuzzled his mouth into the curve of her neck while his hands slid caressingly over the slender curves of her body. 'This would.'

'This,' she gave a bitter little laugh. 'Oh certainly, *this* would, it would have a whale of a time but *this* is only a body, it isn't my mind and afterwards, there'd be nothing left to salvage.'

His voice followed her as she tore herself free of him to go in the direction of the bathroom. 'Don't make too much noise when you come back, I don't like being disturbed.'

When she woke in the morning, she was alone and after she'd showered and dressed, she set about tidying up—folding away the blankets she'd used and then, from habit, everything she found lying about and there was plenty. Piers seemed to dress and undress on the move, leaving a trail of articles scattered wherever he walked. Linnet consoled herself with the thought she wasn't doing it for him but for the benefit of his indoor staff—Matty and the woman who came daily from the village. Last night, after her bath, she'd been depressed—*and I shall find another love* the words had run through her mind, but they'd offered her no comfort. She didn't want kindlier eyes or truer lips and nobody else would ever do.

The couch had been hard but no harder than the camp bed she'd used at the lodge while she was airing mattresses—the dying fire had been warm on her face and she'd watched the glow of it until it all merged into a shining haze. It would have been so easy to slip into the bed beside him and she'd had quite a battle with herself to stay on the couch. At last, she'd been too tired for desire, too tired even to think and she'd fallen asleep knowing the answer to all her questions. Fairy tales didn't come true, at least, not for Linnet Frazer MacArdh!

But morning made things look better and she bounced down the stairs to hear Sheena's voice raised in the breakfast parlour.

'Piers!' It was almost a screech. 'The loneliness here must have affected you. You *can't* do a thing like that.'

Linnet pushed the door open. 'A private fight,' she enquired mildly, 'or can anyone join in?' She looked round the table and what she saw wasn't reassuring. Sheena was obviously in the throes of an icy rage which threatened to overwhelm her superb self control—Piers, in cords and a check shirt looked as though he'd been, very recently, chipped out of flint and Archie appeared to have a king sized hangover. His face was grey and greasy looking, his rather protuberant eyes looked like boiled gooseberries and as she watched, his face took on a greenish tinge, occasioned by Piers thrusting a plateful of bacon and eggs beneath his nose.

Sheena turned to Linnet for support. 'I've just been telling Piers, he can't turn Archie off in this state. You've only to look at him to see he's not fit to travel. You agree with me, Linnie, don't you?'

'He looks like a sea sick billygoat . . .' but she got no further. Piers leaned across the table and threw an envelope on to her plate.

'A letter for you,' he growled. 'The postie brought it here, knowing you weren't at the lodge.'

'Secrets are impossible in the glen,' she turned the envelope in her fingers—one of a pile she'd typed out for Ruby before she left Blackpool but it felt thin. Only one sheet of paper, she guessed as she slit the flap with her knife. One look was enough and she hastily folded the sheet of paper before sharp eyes should see it. 'Must phone at once,' and somehow, she was on the outside of the parlour door and heading for the phone. It wasn't a letter as such, only a scrawl with a felt tipped pen which looked as though it had been done by a very young child. The 'N' was the wrong way round and the four letters which made up the word sprawled all across the page but to her, the word was unmistakable. RING.

Her hands were shaking as she dialled the number and then the piece of paper was twitched from her hand and Piers had it open and was frowning at it. 'You get anonymous letters?' he asked furiously.

Linnet misdialled, pressed down the button and started again. 'No,' her answering whisper was equally furious. 'It's from Ruby.'

'This,' he looked at her disbelievingly, 'this is from

your Miss Ruby Lee?' and his hand stretched out to take the phone from her.

'She can neither read nor write,' Linnet explained in a hurry, she could hear the ringing tone. 'So this must be important. Please go away,' and then Ruby was on the other end of the line and she needed all her attention for the phone.

'Birdie, is that you? Where've you been? I been ringing for two days, I even got the girl at the exchange to ring in case I'd made a mistake. Is anything wrong?'

'Not a thing,' Linnet assumed her most reassuring tone while, over the phone, she leered at her husband. 'I had an invitation,' she explained dulcetly. 'It was so pressing, I couldn't refuse. . .'

'Then that's all right,' Ruby's sigh of relief was breathily audible. 'You had me worried, you not being where you were supposed to be, I hope you're keeping that cottage aired, I don't want to go sleeping on no damp mattresses—— You listening to me, Birdie?'

'Everything's under control,' Linnet answered soothingly while she tried to sound cheerful. This conversation was utterly unlike Ruby who never worried about anything—who always said she didn't have to worry because she knew what was going to happen. A little cold shiver running down Linnet's back forced her into the next words. 'Then why the letter?'

The hesitation in Ruby's voice added to her own disquiet—amplifying it. 'I dunno,' Ruby muttered. 'I just been thinking about you a lot, I suppose.'

'Put it back in its box,' Linnet assumed cheerfulness, 'your crystal ball, I mean and burn your Tarot cards— they're taking you over.'

'I ain't used 'em, not since you been gone. Honest but I been having dreams,' Ruby's voice developed an almost cringing whine. 'You listen to me, Birdie. Believe what I tell you. There's danger for you, danger from horns. I've seen it!'

'Then perhaps I'd better get back to you straight away,' Linnet leapt at the opportunity—it would solve everything. 'I'll pack up and be with you this evening, how's that?'

Over the phone, Ruby's voice came, dramatically solemn. 'You can't run away, Birdie, you ought to know that by now. You stay there, like a good girl and you keep my bed properly aired . . .'

'And the horns?' Linnet forced a giggle, more to set the old lady's mind at rest than anything else. 'Listen, darling, the only horns up here are on the heads of deer and this time of the year, they're no danger to us . . .'

'And you stop mocking me, you saucy little madam—you give the pretty gentleman standing beside you a message from me . . .'

Linnet covered the mouthpiece with her hand and looked at Piers. 'Ruby's having visions,' she mouthed. 'She has a message for you, at least, I suppose she means you, she said "the pretty gentleman standing beside me" '.

'Oh lord!' he groaned. 'Another "sighted" grannie. We'll be starting a coven in the glen. What's the message?'

Linnet made her goodbyes swiftly and hung up. 'Something about the wheel of fortune,' she grinned impishly. 'Ruby's been at the Tarot cards again, but she wants me back at the lodge. I've to keep the beds aired so is it alright with you if I leave after breakfast?'

'So soon?' Piers held on to her hand despite her efforts to get free.

'Mmm, as soon as possible, she says. Thank you so-o-o-o much for your hospitaality, I won't be false and say I've enjoyed every moment but it's not what I'm being paid to do.' And she was aware of a vague disappointment when he nodded understandingly.

'I'll run you over after breakfast—that do?'

Much against her better judgment, Linnet accepted his offer—she could hardly walk the five or six miles round the loch carrying her suitcases. In any case, it was Piers' fault she was here at Eilean Ardh—in the wrong place at the wrong time so it ws really his duty to get her back to where she should be.

Hugging this comforting thought, she blandly accepted his offer to drive her round and when they arrived, she also accepted his offer to chop the kindling for the solid fuel cooker and water heater—bring in the fuel for the fires, light the fires and trim the hedge by the gate while she opened windows, filled hot water bottles and became generally busy. And she didn't ask or explain when she confronted him over an hour later.

'I have to go into Creevie. There's no need for you to wait for me if you've anything pressing. Thank you for your help.' And having said all she intended, she backed her Mini out of the garage and drove off.

It *would* get better, it *had* to get better. One day she'd meet him and the old, familiar wrench at her heart wouldn't be there any more. She'd be able to smile, greet him as an old, not very well remembered acquaintance. The stupidity of the thought brought an almost hysterical laugh to her lips.

She spared a glance for Eilean Ardh, sitting grim and forbidding on the other side of the loch. The sunlight glinted on the tall window of the Room at the top of the round tower—but it had nothing to do with her any longer. She was right off the salvage business!

CHAPTER EIGHT

MOST of the space in Creevie's small car-park was occupied by two large touring coaches—just arrived by the way the passengers were streaming out of them and heading into the town. Linnet parked her Mini and followed the crowd who, from snatches of conversation she heard were touring the Highlands— Fort William, Inverary, Inverewe, Inverness and ending with a couple of days in Edinburgh. She hoped the weather would keep fine for them.

Her shopping done and her string bag bulging, she made her way to the tea shop—if she delayed in Creevie for as long as possible, Piers would have returned to Eilean Ardh by the time she arrived back at the lodge—that was what she hoped—she didn't think she could take much more. Perhaps it would be better to get out altogether and she made tentative plans for a future which would be strictly solo. A seasonal job in an hotel, preferably on the South Coast of England—there might still be vacancies for staff as late as May— She felt an overwhelming irritation to see the tea shop full to the doors.

There wasn't a table, nor even a chair vacant and the two waitresses were rushing madly between the groups of tourists.

'Not a chance, Linnie,' Archie was behind her and murmuring in her ear. 'Not until this lot's back in their coaches. I'm going to try the hotel, they serve morning coffee at the bar. Coming with me?'

Archie, while looking better than he'd done at breakfast still had a very fragile appearance. His colour was bad, his eyes still bloodshot and the hand which he'd put on her shoulder was shaking and weighing heavily as if he needed support. Linnet shrugged and turned from the tea shop with a rueful grimace.

'It looks as if that's my only hope if I want a cup of coffee before I go back, but will they let me in looking like this?' She gestured at her jeans, stained anorak and the bulging string bag.

'They'll let you in,' Archie finicked with his tie and gave her a meaningful leer. 'They can't very well ban Herself of Glenardh, can they? 'S'matter of fact, I'm—er—counting on you to get *me* in—buy me a drink, you know,' and he smiled at her, a poor pathetic effort of a smile but very engaging.

'Poor Archie,' she was understanding. 'Spent up?'

'You know how it is.' He smoothed down his silver blond hair and straightened himself out of his slouch as they entered the hotel and he held the door of the public bar open for her. 'A quality I've always liked about you—you never needed things spelled out for you. To be perfectly honest—and you know how honest I am when I'm sober—I had a drop too much last night and I'm in urgent need. Piers is being awkward, as usual, he's locked everything up and taken the key with him!'

'One small one and a beer for a chaser,' she offered quietly as they seated themselves at a small table in a dark corner. She fiddled in her purse and pressed a five pound note into his hand. 'You order and pay, it'll look better that way.'

'And you leave a fellow a bit of self respect,' he said it admiringly as he examined the note and his pale eyes gleamed hopefully at her.

She shook her head definitely, 'Just one small one, Archie—a beer to follow and a pot of coffee for two,' she stipulated sternly and then softened it with a smile. 'You'll not want to be rolling this early in the day and you know, once you start, you can't seem to stop. Besides, I can't afford any more.'

The coffee came after a short interval, altogether on a tray with the whisky and beer and Archie downed the spirit in one gulp to gaze disconsolately at the glass of beer. 'They'll think I've reformed!'

'And of course, you haven't,' Linnet poured her coffee and chuckled.

'Too late,' he was cheerful about it and rather ingenuous in a bitter way. 'It's one of the few things, perhaps the only thing I do really well. I'm a complete failure at everything else. Did Sheena tell you? She made a nice job for me at Head Office—nothing mind bending, just sitting at a desk and signing things. She called it earning a living—said it was my last chance. Lord! I was so bored, I signed a couple of cheques too many and departed to Florence with the proceeds. I had a whale of a time while the money lasted, but coming back was bloody awful! The way she carried on, you'd think she needed every penny to keep her head above water. You're sure you haven't enough for a real tipple?' He took a sip of beer and grimaced when she shook her head. 'Talking of me reforming . . .'

'. . . which you say you can't . . .'

'. . . I might be able to if I had your help,' he slumped back in his chair. 'If I had you with me, Linnie—if you'd help me, I might just manage it——If you'd come away with me—I'd take you anywhere you liked, Europe, the States and I'd be good to you. I'm not pulling your leg—you could do just as you liked—what I mean is—I wouldn't try to tie you down in any way . . .'

Linnet raised a sardonic eyebrow, watching as he nervously stroked his thin little beard. 'And how much has Sheena offered you to make that suggestion?'

'An extra five thou a year,' Archie was sober, therefore honest, like a child who didn't know right from wrong. 'With my allowance, it'd be enough and I wouldn't bother you—you could . . .'

'. . . I could do just as I liked,' she gazed at him sadly. 'Archie, you've no shame, have you?'

'I can't afford it,' he shrugged his thin shoulders. 'You know Sheena, *she* has the moneybags and I never could manage on my allowance . . . Oh, I see what you mean—it'd cost more to keep the two of us—but I daresay I could get her to up the ante. She's a cold hearted bitch but . . .'

'. . . But she'd pay more to get rid of the two of us?'

'Get rid of you,' Archie was, again completely honest. 'She's got me where she wants me, always has had, ever since Dad died. Well, what d'you say?'

'The same as I said the last time you asked me the same question—more than five years ago.' Linnet made it gentle but firm. 'Nothing doing, Archie. You're not my idea of a husband.'

'But Linnie, I wouldn't expect you to *marry* me!' He was offended she should think such a thing of him and he gave her a wan smile. 'It's too late, kiddo, for anything like that. You'd feel duty bound to try to reform me and you wouldn't have a cat in hell's chance so it wouldn't be fair to tie you down to me. When I'm sober, like now; I *know* I'm an alcoholic and if that isn't a damn good reason for getting drunk, I can't think of a better.'

'Couldn't you go for a cure?'

'Linnie, my little friend, I don't want to be cured,' he finished the beer and at her nod of assent at his unasked question, ordered another to stare gloomily at it when it was brought to the table. 'I go on benders you know—sometimes they last as long as a week—it depends on how much money I have. I'll probably be on one tonight after I've managed to get it over to Sheena that I've failed . . .'

Linnet leaned across the table and touched his hand gently. 'Archie, you haven't failed, not really. There just isn't any point in the plan. Piers could get a divorce from me any time he wanted, I ran away—deserted him.'

'Oh well, I tried.' Archie grinned weakly. 'Let's hope I get that across to her.'

'Yes, you tried,' she gave his hand another pat. 'You can go back and tell your sister, I'll back you up all the way.'

'And we're still friends?' He gulped at what was left of his beer while she poured a second cup of coffee. 'I mean, you understand? There's nothing personal in my not wanting to marry you, not as far as I'm concerned. I just don't think you could take it. That's why I'm not asking, although,' he gave her a sly grin, 'that's not what I'll be telling her. I shall tell her I

offered you my heart and hand and you refused me—
back me up in that, will you?' And at her nod, 'I like
you, I always did, and I never wanted to mess things
up for you. It wasn't *my* idea.'

'I understand,' she stirred thoughtfully at her cup,
'and like I said, I'll back you up, but that portrait,
Archie—who was it originally because I know it
wasn't me.'

'Oh that,' she could tell from the tone of his voice he
hardly remembered, that it was an effort to concentrate, but at last, he got it. 'I was trying my hand at the
Renaissance technique. I always admired it. It was to
have been a copy of a thing by Titian, his "Venus
Anadyamene". Not an exact copy, models aren't so
well built nowadays and I altered the angle of the head
to show nearly a full face. It came out looking a bit like
you, the face, I mean so I made it look a bit more like
you, you've got those quiet Renaissance features—
anyway, Sheena liked it, she gave me fifty guineas for
it and honestly, I didn't see anything wrong with having
it framed and given to you for a wedding present. I know
it wasn't all that good but I was quite proud of it—the
first time I'd ever sold anything I painted. How was I to
know Piers would go off the deep end about it?'

And of course, Linnet understood only too well.
Archie wouldn't have seen anything wrong with it—he
never bothered about things like that. To him, a naked
girl was simply a naked girl, the art galleries of the world
were full of paintings and sculptures of naked girls.

'But why did you tell him afterwards that we . . .
we . . .' She couldn't put it into words but he knew
what she meant and his slack mouth twisted in self
derision.

'I was blotto, darling and my dear sister offered more than I could resist—enough to keep me in Italy for a couple of years. Sorry and all that but you know how I am . . .'

'One other thing,' she pressed him while she could, she might never have the opportunity again—if it was necessary, she was even prepared to buy him some more whisky. 'You *must* have had a model—you said girls weren't that fat nowadays . . .'

'Mmm,' he gave a silly giggle, 'I did!' and at her raised eyebrows, 'Use your head, Linnie. It wasn't a girl from the village, I asked but they wouldn't—you were far too busy with Piers so I used Sheena and the silly bitch insisted on wearing a swim suit so I had to guess about skin tones and things like that. You won't tell . . .'

'No,' she said it as quietly and seriously as if she was taking an oath.

'And you definitely turn down my offer?' He was still hopeful she'd change her mind, he was almost pleading. 'It'd save me one of those dreary scenes and I daresay I could get her to open the purse strings a bit wider . . .'

'No to that as well,' she watched faint hope turn to resignation in his eyes and picked up her shopping bag. She paused for a moment. 'Can I give you a lift back to the village?'

'No thanks,' Archie gave a short, cracked laugh. 'I'll hang on here for a bit, drink the rest of your coffee. You never know, somebody might buy me a dram,' and he hunched his back on her, refusing even to look at her as she went out into the street.

It wasn't until she was nearly halfway back to the

lodge that she realised Archie hadn't given her the change from her five pound note and she smiled in pure self mockery. That, and not disappointment was the reason he'd refused to look at her—or, maybe she was mistaken. Maybe he thought he'd earned it, but she ought not to have made a silly mistake like that. He'd drink until her change was exhausted although it wouldn't last him long, not at the price of whisky. She hoped he wouldn't try to drive his car but it was only a faint hope. Given enough to drink, Archie would have tackled the Eiger in his underwear and without a guide!

If Piers was still at the lodge when she got there, she'd try to delay him for a while, give Archie a chance to sneak in unobserved so there'd be no opportunity for Piers to lose his temper and throw the poor fellow out.

A bit further along, another thought struck her, rather a funny one. All these years, Piers had been working himself into a rage, looking at a portrait—not of herself but of Sheena! Which would be hysterically funny if it wasn't so damn tragic!

The Landrover was parked outside the lodge and deliberately, she parked the Mini so that the two vehicles were bonnet to bonnet and she went into the little house, grinning wryly at her own soft-heartedness—saving Archie, the architect of her own downfall, from Piers—it was enough to make a cat laugh until she managed to establish, in her own mind that Archie hadn't been the architect, he'd only been a not very reliable tool in other hands. Nevertheless, she felt she owed Sheena's brother that much at least and debts must be paid so she smoothed out her face to a pleasant mask and carried her string bag into the kitchen.

'You're still here, good!' she made it sound as though nothing would have pleased her more. 'I'm sorry to be a bit late—have you had lunch?'

'No.' If Piers was astounded or even slightly surprised at her good humour, he concealed it well, merely smiling while he inspected the contents of her bag. 'I've been home to collect a few things I'll need if I'm going to stay here . . .'

Linnet decided at that moment, she was emotionally unstable. All her good intentions vanished like a puff of smoke and irritation flared.

'Then you've wasted a journey,' she snapped. 'This isn't *my* house so I can hardly invite you to stay.' With an effort, she recollected the good intentions and qualified her snappishness. 'The odd meal, perhaps, I don't suppose Ruby would mind about that, but as this is *her* house, not mine, invitations to stay will have to come from her.'

'The odd meal?' He raised his eyebrows. 'Yes, that'll be very welcome. I'll have missed lunch so a share of yours will be welcome.' He grinned at her sardonically. 'Temper, my dear? You should have shared my bed last night—you'd have been more equable, soothed, relaxed . . .'

'Oh, I would have,' her smile tilted her mouth but didn't touch her eyes. 'But the mattress wasn't stuffed with straw and surely, that would be a "must"—I know you like to keep your promises—including all those other threats you whispered in my ear when we had our one and only dance at that delightful wedding party we both attended.' The memory of it made her sick to her stomach, but she conquered the nausea and came up smiling bleakly. 'Will scrambled eggs on toast do?'

He poked about among the packages which he'd laid out neatly on the table. 'Why can't we have pork chops?'

'Because I'm saving them for my dinner tonight.'

'Our dinner tonight,' he corrected. 'I knew, when I brought you here that you'd no intention of returning to Eilean Ardh, that you'd wriggle out of it somehow—and a second kidnapping would be a bore. It wouldn't have the element of surprise which made the previous one so successful . . .'

'Ha!' she broke in on him, 'You wouldn't get the same chance twice . . .'

'Which is just what I've said,' he stopped her in full flight, 'and as for my tenant objecting—I have her permission. If you don't believe me, you know where the phone is.'

'Ruby wouldn't . . .'

'Oh, but Ruby did!' Piers gave her a slow, aggravating smile. 'She has the same ideas I have—we don't like to think of you being here alone—you might have an unwelcome visitor.'

Linnet's mouth dropped open as she gasped with outrage. 'How dare you! Go behind my back, phoning Ruby . . .'

'Mmm,' he agreed. 'Very daring of me, but I thought she ought to be put straight on a certain matter—I like things to be neat and tidy.'

'*You* like,' she snorted with derision. 'So you trot out a sob story. What tale did you tell her, that you were the misunderstood husband? It'd have to be something like that, Ruby's straitlaced,' and at his nod she scowled ferociously. 'I think I hate you.'

Piers shook his head gravely. 'No you don't, mo creadh. Whatever there is between us, it isn't hate.'

No, it wasn't hate, not on her side, she mourned as she reached into the cupboard for a bowl and an egg whisk and at that moment, the sheer stupidity of everything hit her. She broke into a mixture of senseless giggles and tears—but one could easily be blamed on the other.

'You d-didn't like the thought of me alone here at night!' She broke the eggs into the bowl with shaking fingers. 'Here in the glen? You must be raving mad. Unwelcome visitors? Who on earth would walk all this way from the village, along a road which goes nowhere.' A thought occurred to her, 'Did you mean Archie because that makes you madder than ever. Archie'd never hurt or frighten *me* and in any case, I can deal with him, drunk or sober.'

'Easily said . . .'

'. . . and easily done. Sober, you smack his face and he retires to nurse his injured feelings . . .'

'. . . and drunk?'

'Easier still,' she gave him a triumphant and remembering smile. 'If he's drunk, you push him over.' A scornful pity filled her voice. 'He can't get up, you know; he just lies there and goes to sleep.'

'You speak from experience?'

'No more than any other girl in the glen but I suppose you could say that,' she admitted dryly.

'Hardly the young Lochinvar,' she looked up to find his eyes gleaming with laughter and she hooted softly with mockery.

'Young Lochinvar!' Her mockery became tinged with more pity. 'If he leapt to the saddle, he'd miss it. I doubt he could leap to his feet.'

'And you don't dislike him?'

'No, of course not,' she became serious. 'There's nothing there to dislike—he's almost transparent, like glass. If anything, I'm sorry for him—he's weak, easily led and so very lonely.' She inspected the bowl, decided the quantity was too small and reached for two more eggs, laying them on the counter carefully without really seeing what she was doing—her mind on Archie. 'I think it would have been better . . .' she mused aloud and then, remembering her audience, shut her mouth with an audible snap.

'What would have been better?' Piers put a finger under her chin, forcing her face upwards. 'What would have been better, Linnet?'

She twisted her features into a wry grimace—'If Archie'd been born the girl and Sheena, the boy,' she murmured, meeting his eyes squarely. 'A girl can get away with being inadequate—some men seem to like them better that way—if they can't cope. As a matter of fact, I saw him this morning in Creevie, searching for a drink and *no*!' as his brows drew together in a frown, 'It wasn't an assignation, it was quite accidental.'

'If you stare at those eggs any longer, they'll hatch,' Piers changed the subject abruptly. 'Come on, woman, I'm hungry—it's nearly teatime. This is no way, starving me—to start a salvage operation. We're going to use this time to get to know each other again—discover if there's anything left besides the physical attraction between us. A little real caring, maybe. . . .

Something on which we can build a tolerable life together.'

Linnet let him have his say although every word was like a hammer blow at the faint stirrings of hope—she looked into the future and shuddered at what she saw.

'Build a house of sand on rotten foundations?' she muttered. 'A house which'll crumble as soon as I do something you can be suspicious about. A fine sort of life that would be—tolerable, did you say? I'll give you a few days to find out exactly how *in*tolerable it would be!'

Her food stuck in her throat as she tried to eat it and with a grunt, she took her plate across to the kitchen window, opened it and threw the lot outside on to the garden patch—plate and all. 'I'm going for a walk,' she said firmly, watching as he finished eating the makeshift meal. 'I've had all I can stand of your "togetherness" for one day and I don't want you with me.' She was being blunt to the point of rudeness, but what else could she be? She heard his voice as she opened the front door but closed her ears to what he was saying—the time when she'd hung on every word which dropped from his lips was long gone and she obtained a very small amount of satisfaction from slamming the door behind her—hard!

It wasn't that she was running away—she was just removing herself from temptation. A very wise move when her head was telling her not to give in and her body was saying the very opposite. She took a deep breath of cool air and told both body and mind to shut up.

Under the pale April sunshine, the water of the loch was a mild, grey blue, it looked almost asleep and she walked along the edge, scuffing her feet in the silvery sand. A few days and it would all be over—or the worst would be over. As soon as Ruby arrived, she, Linnet would put as many miles between herself and the glen as possible. Like a brute animal in search of a hiding place, she went on grimly until, at the sea entrance to the loch, she climbed up to the top of the ness and dropped to the ground with her back against the gnarled old trunk of a wind warped tree to gaze with dull eyes at the watery waste in front of her.

Today, there was no view of the Isles, even the tip of Trotternish was hidden in haze. Sea and sky seemed to be one, a great curving bowl out of which she couldn't climb. She felt imprisoned here in this world of water, damp mist, heather covered hills, bald mountains, soft spoken people—held fast with no chance of escape. And if she did escape, it would all be there with her in her dreams and she'd wake up with tears on her face as she'd done for the last five years.

But being here, right in the middle of all she loved was far worse than merely dreaming and Piers had changed so much—she hardly knew this big, arrogant, determined man. He wasn't in the least as she remembered him—all the tenderness, the humour and the caring seemed to have been burned out of him. And what he was offering, she couldn't accept, not the sort of life he pictured for her, a lonely, loveless thing with only despair at the end of it. With a sigh, she scrambled to her feet and walked slowly back to the lodge—one part of her dreading seeing him and the other part, equally full of dread that he'd be gone.

It was nearly seven o'clock when she pushed her

way into the kitchen to a mouthwatering odour of grilled pork chops. The table was laid for two and Piers, his best kilt protected by a gaudy, plasticised pinny was performing with a deep fryer and a pile of chipped potatoes.

'Upstairs, bathe and change,' he ordered without lifting his head. 'There's a ceilidh in the village tonight and you're coming with me.'

'I'm not going to any ceilidh,' she thrust out her bottom lip mutinously.

'Yes, you are!' He raised his head from an intent study of the pan of oil and there was no softness in his face. 'If I have to bathe and dress you myself. Don't look like that,' as she let her face harden into stubborn lines. 'It's not the old fashioned type, it's staged and we sit in the audience. There'll be a bit of a dance afterwards, but we needn't stay for that, not if you're ashamed of yourself.'

Linnet straightened from her slouched position. 'Who's ashamed?' she demanded belligerently. 'It's just that I don't see why I have to go when I don't want to.'

'Linnet,' he was patient. 'Glenardh's gone into the tourist business in quite a big way for a such a small place and the people of the glen expect us to back them up—add a touch of glamour to the proceedings. I'm wearing my good kilt and best bonnet so you'll make yourself look equally festive and Old Jamie will walk in front of us. As soon as everybody's had a good gawp, he'll stamp about a bit, playing the pipes, the lights will go out and you can look as bored as you please, but until then, you'll smile—if it kills you. Understand?'

'Perfectly,' she showed her teeth. 'Tell me though, what would you like me to wear—Lovat tweed and cashmere with a hint of heather in my silver mounted grouse claw? Because, my little Scots laird, you'll be dead out of luck . . .'

'You'll wear a smile of radiant happiness,' he snarled, 'as for anything else, I leave that to you although I rather liked the get up I chose for you last night—gay, youthful and it showed your legs which are well worth a second look.'

'You don't mind men looking at my legs?' She made her eyes round with pretended astonishment.

'Not a bit,' he gave her a sly look. 'Looking does no harm at all. It's the "taste and try before you buy" doctrine which makes me mad. Now, hurry up or you'll have to eat a burned offering.'

'And you never tasted or tried,' Linnet retreated to the door.

'Often,' Piers was cheerfully shameless. 'But *not* on the one occasion when I was seriously buying—the whole glen knew that!'

'Double standards,' she spat and whisked herself through the door and upstairs.

After she'd showered, changed and done one or two things to her face, the mirror gave her back a reflection which startled her. According to the glass, she looked happy and eager, very little different from when she'd been nineteen. Her five years away, all her grief—all she'd gone through seemed to have had little effect. Maybe her mouth was a little firmer and there was a wary look in her eyes but that seemed to be all. She pirouetted, making the fullness of the patchwork skirt swirl about her legs—they did look rather nice, especially in the high heeled sandals she was wearing. Then, remembering, she grinned mockingly at her reflection and hurried downstairs, her stomach rumbling and her mouth nearly dribbling as the smell of food reminded her of the meagre diet she'd subjected herself to that day.

As they entered the hall, Linnet stopped, turning to her husband. 'Shouldn't we have picked up Sheena?'

Piers stooped his tall head and she felt his breath tickle her ear and stir some short hairs. 'Don't be daft, Linnet. D'you want everybody to think I run a harem?'

The food had given her courage so that she could smile. 'And you don't, of course?'

'Certainly not,' he was virtuous. 'I'm here, aren't I and my true, wedded wife on my arm. Go along, Jamie,' he nudged the old piper who was waiting for them. 'Make it a grand entrance.'

The lights in the hall were lowered and Linnet sat back in the darkness, caught up in the wild skirl of the pipes, Catriona MacDonald's rich, smooth contralto singing the Spinning Song—a woman from Mull who did 'mouth music' and slowly, she relaxed so that when the performance was over, she could join in the dancing without a thought but to go on enjoying herself.

The fiddles made gay music and she kicked off her sandals to join in 'Stripping the Willow'. It had been a long time since she'd danced like this, whirling down the long lines until she was giddy, to find steadiness and safety in Piers' waiting arms—glad of the support he gave her.

But coming back to the lodge, she was her usual

cool self. The self which had been born five years ago and which she had carefully nurtured ever since. A remote self with a surface like a skin of stainless steel which was a protection and shield against being further hurt. She'd hidden behind that shield, disguising her pain and eventually finding a small measure of immunity but now, the shield was cracked, Piers had shattered it with one look and she was wide open to be hurt again.

He pushed open the door of the lodge and gently but firmly, with a hand in the small of her back, thrust her into the darker darkness of the narrow hallway. Linnet took a deeper breath as the house, warm and somehow welcoming closed around her.

'Do you want anything to eat or drink?' she enquired politely. She might be shivering with alarm but she'd been well drilled in Highland manners— Piers was in this house, a visitor, a guest—no matter how unwelcome—and he had therefore to be treated courteously.

'No,' he switched on the kitchen light and as his arm brushed against her, she shivered again, 'Not food, Linnet although a cup of tea would be welcome—and you?'

'Cup of tea,' she was polite but curt, 'and then I think you'd better go.'

'Only to bed,' his face was impassive but his eyes glinted with purpose. 'I'm staying here, remember?'

Linnet took her courtesy, threw it on the floor and metaphorically, stamped on it before she yawned rudely in his face. 'Is that really necessary.'

'But it's *my* reputation I'm having a care for,' he pointed out.

'Working on the supposition, I suppose that mine's no longer worth saving?' She brought out the words on a sneer. 'Piers, you bore me.'

'Liar!' and at the derision in his voice, she trembled. 'I remember those times very well. Do you want reminding that you were a passionate little thing and it was only will power which prevented me from giving you what you wanted before we married. I could have had it any time and you know it, so don't say I "bore" you.'

'Oh dear,' she drawled. 'How some men fancy their chances and how you must have suffered—so much self denial—faced with temptation and resisting it so nobly.'

'We could make it good if you'd give it a chance,' for a moment she suspected he was almost pleading, but such a thing was unthinkable and she dismissed it as he continued. 'All it takes, Linnet, is a little forgiveness on both sides . . .'

'You're too generous,' she muttered. 'Compassion slopping out of you like water out of a bucket. I don't want you to forgive me, I want you to forget—turn the page—start a new one right from the beginning . . .'

'Linnet,' his deep, soft voice was almost hypnotic. 'Isn't that what I've been suggesting . . .'

'And you'd be willing to take a chance,' she sneered. 'Why?'

'Needs must,' his mouth curved into a wry smile. 'I've discovered that what we had, we still have. At least, it's that way with me.' His arms slid round her, drawing her close and he found her mouth with his own.

Linnet held back for as long as she could, until her own hunger grew too great to be denied and she softened against him. Her eyes slid shut as she felt his tongue gently exploring the softness of her mouth and without thinking, she clung to him to feel his body hardening against her own. It was happening again, as she'd known it would—there was no need for him to hold her, she was doing the clinging, pressing herself against him, almost crying with pleasure as his hands found her breasts—hearing him murmur as they hardened beneath his touch. She thought she'd entered heaven and for one incredible moment she forgot everything—until she heard what he was murmuring against the softness of her throat.

'Linnet, we can still make it good, we *have* to. This time there'll be no more Archies ...' and at that moment, her body, which had seemed to be nothing more than skin containing liquid fire stiffened. The heat died away from her and she became rigid. It wasn't love he was offering, only lust and a way out of the present situation—maybe, he was even saving face—she knew his pride and it must have been badly bruised when she ran out on him.

'No,' it came out as a hoarse, dry mutter. 'I don't want to spend the rest of my life making the best of a bad job ...'

'Tease!' there was a faint flush on his high cheekbones. 'There's a name for women like you ...'

'More than one, I expect,' she pushed herself away from him. 'Go to bed. Recite them all before you go to sleep. You'll feel better in the morning.'

'And you, mo creadh,' Piers' famous temper was on the boil. 'You go to bed as well and if sleep's a long time coming—when you can't bear it any longer, you can knock at my door . . .'

'You forget,' she emptied away the water from the kettle and gave him a withering glance. 'Loneliness doesn't bother me, Piers, I've had five years of it. I'm acclimatised!'

CHAPTER NINE

LINNET rinsed her hands, wiped them dry on the kitchen towel and went to answer the knock on the front door, wondering who it could be. Perhaps it was Catriona again—she'd called once to bring the finished length of her own weaving and she'd promised to come again. But the sight of the green Bentley parked by the wicket gate—the first thing Linnet saw as she opened the door—brought on the old feeling of doom. Sheena, dressed for travel with a blond mink thrown carelessly over her shoulders completed the depression which had settled on her at the sight of the car's long bonnet, although raising one eyebrow and striving to look unimpressed helped her morale a bit.

'Hello,' Linnet's face felt stiff but she forced it into the semblance of a smile. 'I hope you're not looking for Piers—he's not here.' But Sheena didn't take the hint, she just stood there, looking as though she was slumming and didn't care for it. Linnet had no choice—she took a pace backwards. 'Come in,' but it was an unenthusiastic invitation.

Not that Sheena considered she needed an invitation, she stalked past Linnet, pushed open the door to the sitting room, said, 'This will do admirably. Come in and close the door behind you, Linnie,' and seated herself, without another glance in Linnet's direction.

Linnet didn't close the door, she hovered, undecided what to do.

'Tea?' she offered bravely while something told her that this was the crunch and she didn't feel up to it.

Piers had stayed in the lodge for three days and nights and the nights had been the worst. During the daylight hours, he was out most of the time—visiting the remote crofts scattered about the uplands— overseeing the work on the farm at the head of the glen—discussing business with his factor but evenings, they were bad. The house seemed to seal itself round the two of them, making everything closer, more intimate. He'd hardly spoken and she'd tried desperately to pretend he wasn't there but her mind refused to allow him to sink into obscurity. He *was* there and his very presence was a temptation.

Sheena watched the hovering and a tight smile curved her lips fractionally. 'I've come to say goodbye, Linnie. I'm leaving for Edinburgh. Of course, I shall be back in time for May Day but I hope you'll have seen sense by then—I'm almost sure you will have.'

'Sense?' Linnet recovered a little of her aplomb. 'You're talking over my head, Sheena. I'm a very simple person, too simple to understand innuendos. You'll have to put it in plain English and in words of not more than two syllables. What sense is it you want me to see?'

Sheena's patrician nostrils thinned with exasperation. 'Sense, Linnie. Pounds and pence, to be brutally frank . . .'

'. . . Which you are . . .'

'. . . Don't interrupt!' For a moment, Sheena's composed mask slipped and Linnet caught the gleam, the hard glitter of anger but it was gone, almost before she identified it and the cool, composed mask was back in place.

'Five years ago, Linnie,' Sheena opened her handbag and took out a handkerchief, increasing the cloud of Chypre which had entered the room with her—'Five years ago, I made a mistake,' she shrugged. 'Perfectly natural, of course—I left Piers' fantastic determination out of my calculations. Oh, I knew all about you and him but I reasoned that once he'd had what he wanted, your little affair would die the death—but it didn't. He married you—some latent chivalrous instinct, I suppose. It wasn't what his mother wanted for him and it wasn't what I wanted either—it wasn't practical. So I felt quite justified in doing my best to put a spoke in your wheel. Archie's— er—*tendre* for you, his habit of putting your face on anything he painted was a god-send and I didn't grudge the money it cost me—either to buy the painting, have it framed or get Archie to tell the tale I wanted. It cost me a pretty penny altogether, but as I said, I didn't begrudge it . . .'

'. . . Which is all ancient history . . .' Linnet broke in.

'. . . And you should have left it that way,' Sheena drawled but once again, the glitter showed for just a split second. 'You're reasonably intelligent . . .'

'Thanks,' Linnet was dry—her voice and her mouth felt and sounded like last year's leaves, desiccated, but Sheena paid no attention to the interruption. She was intent and quite dispassionate.

'Don't thank me, I take the long term view—it's my nature. I'm first and foremost a business woman, a very successful one and sentimentality doesn't sway me—I've always found it tends to cloud the issue. I think marriage should have a good, solid foundation,

like a business, don't you?' And without giving Linnet
a chance to voice an opinion—it wasn't necessary—
Sheena placed no value on anybody's opinion but her
own, she continued smoothly.

'When I say "solid", I mean just that. Financially
sound—plenty of available capital to see one over the
bad times, if and when they come.' Sheena could have
been presenting her plans for setting up a new chain of
supermarkets to her board of directors for all the
emotion she displayed, but Linnet didn't interrupt,
she waited. The crunch was coming and she felt the
hair prickle on the back of her neck.

'Archie says you've discussed my proposition . . .'

'. . . And rejected it!' Linnet felt good saying that.

'Mmm,' Sheena inclined her head graciously. 'That
shows I was right about you, you're not such a dreamy
little fool as you look. Archie hasn't much time left
and of course, when and if anything happens to him,
the allowance would cease.'

Linnet felt something very like hate rise in her
throat—it was bitter enough for hate. 'That's your
own brother you're talking about so casually. Don't
you care what happens to him?'

Sheena looked at her blandly. 'Not much. As a
brother, he's something of an embarrassment, an
expensive embarrassment. You should have been
sensible and taken what I offered. Now, if he drinks
himself to death—in a way, it'll be your fault, not
mine. You wouldn't be able to stop him but you might
have delayed the end—he was always a fool about you.'

'Oh no,' Linnet made a gesture with her hands,
pushing away a sickening thought. 'You're not going
to lay the blame for Archie's condition on me!'

Sheena crossed her ankles, studied her handmade shoes with a critical eye and after apparently deciding they were worth what she'd paid for them, she raised her head to give Linnet almost a malicious smile.

'No, my dear, I shan't blame you, I shan't have to. You'll blame yourself, you're that type. Always you'll be wondering—quite pointlessly whether or not it *was* your fault. But that's all by the way. I've changed the terms of my proposition. You don't have to go off with Archie—the money's yours provided you go. I'm prepared to be quite generous—I'm always prepared to pay for what I want . . .'

'. . . and you want . . .?'

'I want Piers,' Sheena said it coolly. 'He's mine and I want him back! You've had five days with him, three of them alone here in the lodge, that should have been quite long enough for him to get you out of his system—I've given you that time together—I think I've been more than generous in that respect so, be sensible, Linnie. Take what I'm offering and be grateful. Show your gratitude by not making a fuss when my legal firm gets in touch with you. Make it easy on all of us, we don't want to be involved in any more scandals.'

Linnet felt swamped—as if she'd once more fallen into the loch and the water was rising to cover her mouth and nose, stifling her, drowning her but something inside of her held together, telling—insisting she kept calm.

'You've plans?' She heard herself say the words and marvelled that she should sound disinterested.

'Of course,' Sheena was impervious to atmosphere and Linnet knew she was generating one hell of a lot of it. 'Since Piers is set on this tourist thing, I propose to see it's done properly. For instance, I shall have all this side of the loch for a chalet development, I've already had quotes from a firm which specialises in the Norwegian and Swedish type. Not too many, of course, I don't want to spoil the view from Eilean Ardh. Then there'll be the construction of a decent marina, somewhere for the yachts to berth and lay over during the winter. I'll have my people vet the customers thoroughly—we'll want to keep out the riff raff. I assure you, Piers will be quite satisfied with my plans,' her voice sharpened, became almost strident. 'That's what I can do for him, Linnie. That and bring Eilean Ardh up to scratch, restore it to its former state—you *must* have noticed how dilapidated it's become. It really needs a huge injection of capital—I can do that for him whereas, you can do nothing except stand by his side while his home rots around him because neither you nor he have the money to keep it as it should be kept.'

It was a long speech and at the end of it, Linnet felt breathless, just listening but from somewhere she found the strength to reply.

'And if Piers doesn't care if it rots—if he'd be quite happy living in an ordinary house . . .'

'Linnie,' Sheena raised her eyebrows. 'Piers live in an ordinary place—one of those patio conversion things in the village! Don't be a fool. Can you see him in a place like that? Besides, Eilean Ardh is the family home, the MacArdhs have held it for centuries. He'd be like a fish out of water anywhere else. He wouldn't be happy and you know it. Now, be a sensible girl and accept my offer, if not for your own sake, for Piers'.'

Linnet took a deep breath. 'I'll think about it,' she murmured.

'Good,' like a mistress dismissing a scruffy housemaid, Sheena rose to her feet, collected her mink which had slipped from her shoulders and laid it carefully over her arm. The hand she extended to Linnet was not for shaking, it held a small piece of pasteboard. 'My telephone number, I'll be expecting to hear from you, but make it soon, I'd like everything cleared up quickly so that I can get well ahead with my plans.' And as if they'd been discussing something of no more importance than the price of tea, she walked gracefully out to her car.

Linnet went back to the kitchen, her nerves screaming with tension and her hands and legs shaking. She slumped into a chair, put her elbows on the table, her head in her hands and burst into the tears of reaction. Not that she'd ever considered she had any hope, not real hope but always, deep inside her, the hope had lived. Anything else, she could have fought but not this cold calculation of Sheena's—this reduction of everything to the basic pounds and pence. As though men, women and their hopes and desires had no value against money.

When she judged her hands were steady enough to hold things, she wiped the last traces of tears from her face and made herself a pot of tea, adding a generous splash of whisky to her cup—too much, she thought as the mixture of tea and scotch hit her stomach, but it served to chase away the dull lethargy from her brain and she could think clearly once more.

The point was—Linnet hesitated while her brain fought through the maze of ifs and buts—the point was that she *knew* Piers wanted her. He made no attempt to hide it—it was there in the tone of his voice, in his touch and in the way he kept insisting that they had something of the old feeling still between them and as he had said several times, why shouldn't they try to make the best of things.

Her own reluctance would have crumbled on the first day if she could have been sure of his motives—sure that he wasn't doing it more to salve his pride than for any other reason—if, instead of all the blather about salvage, he'd said he still loved her—and meant it, of course.

And another point—one she fastened on greedily because it made her feel better—Sheena *must* be worried, otherwise she wouldn't offer so much money just to get rid of a nonentity like Linnet Frazer. As she took her cup and saucer across to the sink, she caught sight of herself in the small mirror which hung on the wall beside it—puffy eyes with shadows beneath them—traces of tears on her cheeks and a long smear by the side of her nose. 'You look a fright,' she told herself, jerking with surprise as her voice rang round the room—she hadn't realised she was speaking aloud and with a swift inspection of the casserole in the oven—it was doing nicely, it would be ready for lunch—she fled upstairs to rectify her appearance.

Piers came in at one o'clock, standing just inside the kitchen door, a small smile curling his firm, closed mouth as he raised his nose and sniffed audibly.

'Beef casserole,' Linnet enlightened him. 'Perfectly safe to eat, I had second thoughts and left out the arsenic.'

'I wasn't sniffing that,' he crossed to the table and

inspected the neat arrangement of cutlery. 'I could smell Sheena. What did she want?'

'You, I expect,' Linnet bent down in front of the oven, more to hide her face than to remove the dish. 'She was leaving for Edinburgh—but she's coming back for May Day.' She put the casserole on the table and gestured to it. 'Help yourself, don't bother about me, I had a sandwich for my elevenses and it's spoiled my appetite.' A plan was emerging in her brain, she could see the overall shape of it and wanted to get away somewhere by herself to work out the details, but first, she had to know something and it didn't matter if Piers thought her a mercenary bitch, she had to ask.

'Regarding this—er—salvage operation,' deliberately, she leaned back against the dresser and made her voice and face very composed—the voice especially—to her ears it sounded almost businesslike. 'Can you afford a penniless wife, Piers?'

'Just,' he was imperturbable as he ladled the steaming, savoury smelling contents of the casserole on to his plate. 'Do I take it you're beginning to take me seriously—you've stopped playing for time?' He was seated and consequently had to look up at her but even with that slight advantage over him, Linnet felt vaguely uncomfortable. His next words increased her feeling of discomfort.

'In that case,' she could see little flames glowing at the back of his eyes. 'I propose that, since Sheena's left, we both go over to Eilean Ardh when I've finished up this evening and start again where we left off five years ago.'

Linnet put her hands behind her, squeezing her

fingers together until she could feel them going numb—it hurt but it prevented her from screaming. 'Don't you think that would be pushing things a bit?' She heard herself saying the words and was pleased with the 'throw away' tone she managed to infuse into them.

He muttered something in Gaelic and then translated for her benefit. 'Equivalent to "Strike while the iron's hot" or "No time like the present" even "Procrastination is the thief of time", and it'll settle all the speculation in the glen. Things here will settle down at last.'

Perhaps, if he'd abandoned his meal and taken her in his arms, she'd have felt better about it. If he'd kissed her, she'd have kissed him back, gone willingly and forgotten Sheena, forgotten the whole world, but Piers did nothing like that. He merely gave her a small, closed smile and went on eating. And when he'd finished and—she looked glumly at the table—he'd eaten everything in sight—he gave her an approving pat on the shoulder and went upstairs.

A quarter of an hour later, he came down, changed from jeans and anorak into kilt, a clean white shirt and a leather patched tweed jacket. He didn't look over the moon with delight or anticipation, he didn't even touch her, just gave her another tight smile before he explained his change of dress.

'I'm off to Gairloch,' he occupied his hands with checking the contents of his plain, undecorated sporran before he started on his pockets, almost as though he didn't want to touch her. 'We had a message from one of the boats, engine trouble and it's putting in there so while I'm gone, pack your things, mo creadh and be ready to leave.'

'Ruby said . . .'

'Ruby will understand,' he cut her off short.

Linnet watched the Landrover go off from the sitting room window while all the time, something inside her was screaming *No! Not like this!* He'd slapped his bonnet on his head at a cocky, arrogant angle and gone without a backward glance but she'd imagined triumph and self satisfaction in every step he'd taken down the short garden path. Typically male, she raged—no understanding, no love, no nothing! and she fled upstairs, dry eyed and shaking with misery. She would go but not to Eilean Ardh. She'd go to Ruby, stay over a day, explain things and then lose herself in some other busy resort, somewhere nicely crowded where she'd be like an ant, among thousands of other scurrying ants. Gradually her plans formulated—*not* take the Mini—*not* go by the road to Creevie, not even walking along it. Eyes used to looking into distances, eyes which could distinguish an individual sheep a mile away would have no difficulty in seeing her and tongues which relayed every morsel of information would pass the word—she doubted if she could even walk along the road to the village without it being commented on . . .

Running away again? No, she was merely retiring to a more strategic position. She'd got over him once, in a way and she could do it again. Any amount of loss would be better than what he was offering—if she took that, she'd hurt for the rest of her days. There was one way she could go even if she didn't have darkness to hide her—and she couldn't afford to wait for night to cover her escape—the hard way. Leave at dusk; Piers wouldn't, couldn't be back before then—slip in among the pines until she was well past Glen Ardh, climb the lower slopes of Beinn Ardh, go round the shoulder of the mountain, skid down the scree, as she'd done often when she was younger into the narrow defile which separated the Beinn from the uplands—climb up and walk across the peaty moor until she reached the road which ran from Creevie to Achnasheen. Here, she could hitch a lift into Achnasheen itself and have a choice of bus or train to Inverness.

A nine mile hike, she would allow herself four hours but that would mean arriving at the road too late to hitch a lift—Linnet solved that problem by remembering the MacNeills' croft which was about two miles from the road, down a track. The MacNeills, an old couple had left the place—gone to live with a married daughter in Ullapool—Piers had mentioned it. He'd also said that the single storeyed croft was used now as a shelter for shepherds and such until he could find a buyer for it. He'd made a face about that—few people wanted a two roomed croft in such an isolated and exposed spot, but meanwhile it was being kept in good repair. Which meant it would be dry, and if it was used by shepherds and such, those sort of men would keep a few things there for their comfort—she would stay there the night and use the comforts provided, and she had no fear of walking or of finding the croft already occupied—it was too early in the year for any sheep to be grazing that high.

Automatically, she washed up Piers' dinner dishes and tidied the kitchen before she went up to her room and stuffed—as she stuffed once before—a spare pair of jeans, a shift and some underwear into a large shoulder bag. Events were repeating themselves, but this time it would be better. There would be no jagged rocks to scramble over and best of all, no haste, no need for it. She had time to plan, time to do things methodically. There would be no signs of her departure even.

When she'd put everything ready, even leaving her nightie over the back of the bedside chair as though she was going to use it—and her few bits of makeup grouped tidily on the dressing table—she swung open the door of the wardrobe—no clues there—it all looked very much as usual, she slipped out of her shoes and stretched herself on the bed.

A nine mile hike when she hadn't walked that far for five years would be strenuous, to say the least and she wanted to be fresh for it.

The sun was just setting as she slipped out of the house, rather pleased with her last act which had been to write a simple message on the scribbling pad and leave it on the table in full view so that Piers wouldn't miss it when he eventually came back. *Gone visiting* and signed with a defiant *L.F.* That should hold him for a while, he'd sit and wait for her to return. She gave a little, almost hysterical giggle. He'd probably go into his 'Highland Chieftain' act and pack her things for her.

There was a thick haze over everything, she couldn't even see the sea entrance of the loch and the loch water itself had a strange look, as though it wasn't water but a great expanse of molten lead—not a ripple on the surface. From Eilean Ardh came the sound of the pipes—Old Jamie doing his nightly stint at being MacArdh's piper—tramping up and down what remained of the walls and playing his lament. His own composition which had won prizes at various Games and of which he was very proud. 'Lament for a Prince'—she heard the sweetly sad, sobbing melody above the drone of the chanters, the grace notes almost trickling in the still air and she snorted to herself with exasperation. That Prince had gone over the water more than two hundred years ago, never to return and yet, he was still lamented—Celtic memory! As she dodged into the shadows of the pines, her feet crunching on the dry, fallen needles, the Lament came to an end and Jamie started up on 'Amazing Grace' and she heard herself softly singing it. '*Was bound but now, am free.*'

Linnet's eyes filled so that pines and shadows blurred and ran together. What a hope! Always she'd be bound to this place and to Piers. They'd be in her mind, in her heart until the day she died—she'd never be free. Even if she at last managed to find some small happiness for herself, even if she lived day by day in the outside world, she'd dream of the glen and wake with tears on her face and an aching heart for what never could be.

An old, old memory tugged at her giving her a feeling of unease and it wasn't until the wind sprang up that she remembered Uncle Fergie's weather prophesying—'Still air, still water, stay at home', and she recalled the still surface of the loch, the way Jamie's piping had floated across and nervously, she fiddled with the zip of her anorak. There hadn't been a breath of breeze when she'd left the lodge, everything had been too still, as though the whole glen was waiting for something—she could feel the wind freshening against her cheek as she walked out from the shelter of the pines and started her climb up the smooth slope. There was a storm coming but it wouldn't be here yet. It had to wait until she was well away and she wondered wryly if praying would do any good.

Before she'd rounded the shoulder of Beinn Ardh, the storm was upon her, heavy clouds obscuring the thin moon and her small torch wasn't of much use so that her progress was slowed. She was already nearly half way to her destination, the croft, and it seemed stupid to turn back now and since she'd taken over two hours to cover the four and a half miles this far, she calculated it would be quicker and more sensible to push on.

That was before she lost her footing on the scree and slid, on her rear to the bottom to land in the rain swollen burn which flowed down the defile. She scrambled out of the water and on to the bank, trying to find some cover from the driving rain and shuddering in the chill night air. She was soaked to the skin already but the cold burn water had numbed her bruises and since there was no shelter, she tackled the steep incline grimly, finding footholds and handholds in the dark—she'd need her torch for later.

By the time she'd reached the flat highland, the rain had turned the peaty ground into a gluey consistency which clung obstinately to her feet when she sank into it and perversely, she seemed to have lost her sense of direction. Wearily, she trudged on, the rain and the driving wind at her back—that way, she knew she was heading in roughly the right direction until she stumbled into a ditch and when she'd dragged herself out of it, she was on the road—she'd come too far and missed the croft altogether.

But the road was better for walking on and within five hundred yards of where she'd joined it, she found the track which led down to the croft and with a sigh of relief, she stumbled along, the gale force wind driving rain into her face so that she almost ran into the place.

All she wanted to do, when she'd closed the door behind her was to sink down somewhere and, preferably, die but there were other things more important. First of all, she'd light a fire, search for anything useful—she thought wistfully of the casserole which she'd refused to eat at lunch time and the thought of it made her mouth water.

The torch battery was nearly exhausted and by its fading light she found a candle, matches in a water proof tin, tea, sugar—also in waterproof tins, two thick mugs, a spoon and an unopened tin of condensed milk. On the high, old fashioned mantelpiece over the fire place there was an oil lamp which she shook gently, smiling with relief as she heard the oil sloshing about in it and when she'd lit it, she discovered that what she'd thought was rubbish in the fireplace was actually kindling and there was a bucket of peats set ready in the hearth.

Before she lit the fire, she filled the kettle from the rainwater butt at the corner of the tiny building and when the fire was going nicely, she inspected the remainder of the place. There wasn't much of it, two rooms, of which this, the living room, was the biggest—a curtained-off alcove occupied one third of it but when she pushed the heavy old curtain aside, there was no bed. That had been removed and in its place, on the floor was a thin palliasse and a couple of rough wool blankets. It wasn't much but infinitely preferable to spending the night on the floor.

After a cup of tea, milkless because she had nothing which would open the can of milk, she stripped, hung her wet things on a string line under the mantelpiece, wrapped herself in one of the blankets and, dragging the palliasse from the alcove to a good position in front of the fire, she lay down and pulled the other blanket over her. There was no pillow and her lips curved in a tired smile as she recalled the story of a long ago young chieftain who had come home from his schooling in France to lead his clan. It had been winter time and the young man had made a huge snowball, patted it into shape and rested his head against it to sleep while the clansmen had murmured in distress. What sort of youth was this whom they would be following—a boy who couldn't sleep without a pillow!

As for herself, the softest, downiest pillow in the world wouldn't have made her sleep, even though she was so tired. Little pieces of her personal puzzle were clicking into place at last and what she saw now as an over all picture made her far from happy.

The first time she'd run away, frightened as she had been, deep within her had lain the hope that Piers would come after her. She hadn't admitted such a thing of course—any time during the past five years, she would have denied it stoutly, but it had been there always—that tiny hope he'd find her and everything would be all right, that they'd be together again somehow. But this time was different, this time, she was going and hope was dead—the last little glimmer of it had gone out when she'd left the lodge. This time, she'd cut herself free and the thought didn't bring either comfort or happiness.

CHAPTER TEN

THE sound of an engine and the rumble of wheels, the wet spattering sound of tyres brought Linnet upright in her makeshift bed to gaze, horrified at the door which she had forgotten to bolt—anybody could get in. She swore rudely at her own stupidity—she hadn't even extinguished the lamp and the croft could be clearly seen from the road, even more so at night if there was a light shining through the unshuttered windows. There was the squeal of brakes, the silence when the engine was cut and in that silence, the slam of a car door before somebody tried the door of the croft—tried it, found it wasn't secured and roughly pushed it open.

'What the hell are you playing at, Linnet?' Piers stood just inside the door, rain spattered and looking as though he was searching for a good fight. 'I've been phoning the lodge at quarter hour intervals from Gairloch . . .'

'Sorry you've been put to the trouble,' she wrapped herself in as much dignity as possible—which wasn't a lot. It was hard to be dignified when one was lying on the floor and one's only covering was a couple of blankets. She was exasperated with herself—she didn't seem to be able to do anything right. 'Oh, for heaven's sake come in and shut the door—having it open like that's making the fire smoke.'

Piers closed the door quietly and she took it as a

warning that he was more than in a temper. 'Gone visiting!' he raged at her. 'Another lie—you haven't gone visiting at all. I went to nearly every house in the village, you weren't in any of them and as for that L.F. you signed—you haven't been Linnet Frazer for five years. You're Linnet MacArdh and don't you forget it!' He stalked across to the fireplace, felt the garments which she'd hung up to dry and bent to examine her shoes—'You walked! Why didn't you use your car?'

Linnet had recovered herself. 'You know how it is,' she was airy. 'A fine evening, I went for a walk. I just went a bit farther than I intended . . .' While she was speaking, she surreptitiously tried to cover her bulging shoulder bag with a corner fold of one of the blankets but he pounced on the thing and despite her angry protest, opened it to display her slightly damp change of clothes.

'Running away again?' He raised a dark eyebrow at her and in the shadows cast by the oil lamp, his features showed a devilish cast, long chin, aquiline nose and broad forehead highlighted and his cheeks shadowed to gauntness. 'Why?' He asked it softly. 'I can't recall threatening you this time. As I remember, we had a very civilised discussion about it and I felt we were getting somewhere at last. There wasn't any need for you to take to the hills.' He shook his head at her gravely, 'A walk on a fine evening!—Linnet, you little idiot. Every weather forecast has been promising this storm and you start on a nine mile hike! What were you going to do?'

'Hitch a lift into Achnasheen in the morning,' she muttered, 'Get a bus or a train to Inverness . . .'

'. . . and back to Blackpool with your tail between your legs?'

'I was going there first,' she admitted. 'After that—who knows?'

'And all because I was pressurising you a bit,' again, he shook his head at her, and changed the subject abruptly. 'You've had a cup of tea, I see. D'you want another?'

'Mmm, it would be nice,' she stifled a sigh of relief that he'd stopped asking awkward questions, the last thing she wished to talk about were her motives. 'Have you got one of those Boy Scout's knives with a thing on it to open tins—I had to drink my tea without milk because I'd nothing to open the can, only a nail file and I don't like tea without milk—it makes my mouth feel furry.' And as he rose to put the kettle back on the fire, 'How did you know I'd be here?'

'Elimination.' Linnet had a side view of his face as he said it and she watched his mouth curve into a small closed smile—almost of satisfaction. It didn't take away the severity or completely banish the sternness but it softened it so that he looked less flinty. Almost hypnotised, she went on watching his face and the flickering emotions which crossed it while he explained.

'You weren't anywhere in the glen—after I found that note, we searched as thoroughly as we could. Your car was still at the lodge so you hadn't driven yourself away. You hadn't walked up the road to Creevie—I made enquiries about that so you had two choices. You could have gone with Archie or you could have gone this way.'

'Brilliant!' Linnet was as nasty as she dared be—her

present position didn't leave her much latitude in that respect. 'Your mind would fly automatically to Archie—you've got a thing about him.'

'As you say,' he didn't dispute it, 'I have a thing about him—once bitten, twice shy—but fortunately, Archie'd left much earlier, not long after Sheena and he was noticed—not too sober, I suppose, probably driving carelessly, but he was alone in the car.' Piers' black eyebrows made a straight bar across the top of his hawk-like nose and now, there was no curve to his mouth, it was a straight, thin line. 'If you'd gone off with Archie, my girl, I'd have followed and caught up with you somehow and this time, I *would* have killed him!'

'This time?' She said it wonderingly and Piers snorted as he fetched the other mug from the cupboard.

'You don't think he got off scot free before, do you? I had to wait until the shindig was over and everybody'd gone,' his hands curled and he grinned as though he was contemplating a particularly pleasant memory. 'It was just as well I threw him down the stairs before I discovered *you* were gone as well—otherwise he'd have fallen a lot harder and it would have been all the way—top to bottom—instead of just three or four steps. It was a mild lesson to teach him to keep his hands off my property!'

Linnet forgot caution. 'Your property!' Her voice rose in an indignant squeal. 'I'm *not* your property!'

'Oh yes, you are,' his deep voice cut across her shrillness, its quiet firmness silencing her. 'You're mine, my girl.'

She wagged her head at him, trying to look dignified

and untouchable. 'Not after the things you said to me that night *and* the things you've said, the names you've called me since I came back . . .'

'Be quiet!' The words cut her off in mid flight; he hadn't shouted but there was an authority there. 'Just listen for a change,' he went on. 'Listen for once instead of being too busy thinking up your next insult. We, you and I got off to a good start but something went wrong along the way—I was as much to blame for that as anybody and I admit it—but we've got to put it right and start again. I was going to do that tonight,' he glanced round the tiny, cheerless room and his nose wrinkled. 'Not here, mo creadh, I wanted better for us than this but fate's taken a hand so we'll make this do. It's the way I want it, the way you want it. Don't shake your head like that. The time, the place and the loved one all together . . .'

Linnet's eyes widened in apprehension as he undid buttons and his shirt followed his jacket to make the beginnings of a pile on the floor. She closed them tightly and shuffled herself round with her back to him as he started on the leather straps which fastened his kilt. She could feel her hands becoming cold and damp with perspiration and when she looked down at them, pale against the dun colour of the blanket, they were visibly trembling. The sound of his soft step and the deepening of the shadows in the room told her he was turning down the lamp and she made a desperate bid for delay.

'You've transport, shouldn't we get back to the glen?' Her voice was a bit shrill but steady enough, under the circumstances.

The lamp flickered, she heard the puff of air as he

blew down the glass chimney to extinguish the remains of the flame and then he was beside her, parting the blankets and she felt cool, smooth skin against her own and hands which caressed—warm hands with long, strong fingers, a finger drifted across her face and in the darkness, found her lips and laid itself across them gently.

'No, we don't go back before morning,' he'd lowered his head and he was murmuring it into the hollow behind her ear while he nuzzled away the fall of her hair. 'We're going to settle this now, here where we shan't be disturbed.'

'No,' her teeth were gripped on her bottom lip and she moaned between them as he turned her to face him. 'No Piers, please. Not like this ... Not in hate ...'

'You didn't listen!' She caught the accusing tone but it was softened by a short, breathy laugh as he stroked the blanket away from her shoulders. 'I said "Loved one". Hate and love, two different sides of the same coin, my heart, and either is better than indifference. We're not indifferent to each other, if we were, we couldn't hurt each other so much ... Linnet, this is the way it *must* be.'

Linnet lay very still as his hands worked their magic, his mouth following the feathery touch of his fingers and as always, the old flame sprang to life inside her, the heat of it growing and spreading to steal through her whole body. In times past, when she'd been young, before they'd married, Piers had controlled that flame—never allowing it to burst into a blaze but he wasn't controlling it now, he was encouraging it so that it licked through her, turning her molten, making her soft against him—soft, willing and wanton.

She heard his voice, not words she knew—he'd dropped into an older, sweeter, softer language which she'd never been able to learn or speak but language no longer mattered. His head was a dark shape against the dim fireglow, there was no expression for her to read or misread; only the feel of him against her, muscle and sinew in a smooth covering of skin pressing, demanding and tormenting until, with a cry which was almost a sob, she felt her last scrap of resistance crumple and she no longer had any power to deny him anything he wanted.

Her hands reached out and twisted in his hair before they slid to his shoulders, her nails scoring at skin which felt like silk beneath her fingertips and through the thunder of the blood beating in her ears she heard his murmur of approval and encouragement. The pain was nothing to her, only like watching a long delayed sunrise and her little cry was stifled against his chest before she was bathed in a glory almost too bright and beautiful for her senses and she clung desperately to him while the world fell away and there were only the two of them left in the whole universe. Gently, she floated back down to earth again, turned her face into the cool dampness of his shoulder and slept, secure in the curve of his arm.

'Linnet,' a finger gently tapping at her cheek woke her. It was morning, very early morning judging by the thin, pale light outside the tiny, deepset window and Piers was at her side with a mug of tea. Without thinking, she smiled at him before she noticed the grimness about his mouth. It struck cold to her heart and her hands shook as she struggled an arm free of the warmth of the blankets and took the mug from him. What had she done wrong now?

'So,' his tone was as grim as his face. 'So Archie lied?'

Linnet buried her nose in her mug, took a sip of scalding tea, raised her head long enough to say 'Yes,' and lowered it again.

'Why didn't you tell me?' he demanded roughly.

A tealeaf had floated to the surface and she watched as it made a slow, lazy circle before she raised her head again to meet his angry eyes.

'You're not the only one with pride,' she said it quietly. 'I've a bit myself. Archie lied—you believed the lie—if you believed that of me, what was the use of going on . . .'

'If you hadn't run away, I'd have found out for myself . . .'

Linnet shook her head wearily. 'How was I supposed to know that!' She made a small, exasperated noise in the back of her throat, took another gulp of tea and raised pain filled eyes to his. 'Remember, I didn't have a mother to tell me things—only Uncle Fergie and he wasn't much good when it came to explaining the facts of life. He tried once,' her mouth curved into a rueful smile as she remembered. 'It wasn't easy for him to explain and I was no wiser when he'd finished than when he started. It was all "ers" and "ums" and "you know what I mean, lassie". I didn't even know you could tell, not then! It wasn't until much later I found out about it and that was from a book.' She pulled a face, 'And the book didn't go into detail. All I could see, when you looked at me was distrust and I didn't think I could live with that—you not trusting me. Everything felt dirty and spoiled . . .'

'So you ran away,' he nodded as though her garbled explanation was quite satisfactory. 'But last night, Linnet, you knew yet you ran away again. Why?'

Linnet remained silent—his face wasn't a closed book to her any longer—she could look at him and almost see what he was thinking. The clues were slight, a tensing of his facial muscles, the suspicion of a frown, a twitch at the firm corners of his mouth. She should have seen all this before—or was it something which had grown during the night—opening her eyes—or perhaps she'd been wilfully blind.

Piers shook her gently. 'Why?' he repeated the question and when she still didn't answer, he allowed himself a guess.

'Something Sheena said when she called yesterday morning?'

Quietly, she muttered a muffled 'Yes', surprised that it was only yesterday. It all seemed so very far in the past—it could have been years ago.

'Then I know what it was,' his mouth had taken a wry curve as though he'd tasted something bitter. 'The old story, enough truth to make it believable and a bit of exaggeration. I'm a pauper, aren't I? I'm hanging on to my house and my land by the skin of my teeth. I need a rich wife to make things easy for me. Did she tell you her plans for the glen—the chalets, the marina for the yachts of the wealthy? Was that how it went?'

'Something like that,' she agreed, unwilling even now to make any trouble.

'And not so far from the truth that I could call her a liar,' his mouth broke into a reluctant grin, rueful and full of self mockery. 'I'm not rich, my heart; I can't wrap you in mink or shower you with diamonds but I'm not a pauper . . .'

'I never wanted anything like that,' she broke in fiercely. 'I never even thought about it but,' she became mournful, 'Sheena could give you so much, make everything easy . . .'

'Buy me?' He took the mug from her unresisting fingers and placed it carefully on the flagged floor. 'My god, Linnet, do you think I'm that sort of man? I want neither Sheena nor her money, I've got the wife I want and enough to keep her in modest luxury. The glen's self supporting, it's even beginning to show a small profit . . .'

'Oh stop it,' she clenched her fits and hammered them against his chest. 'I *told* you, I don't care. I don't want mink or diamonds, I've never even thought about them. I just wanted . . .'

'I know what you wanted, my love,' he looked down at her tenderly. 'You wanted what I wanted—for us to love each other, live together . . .'

'How did you know about the chalets and things,' she asked suspiciously, still not sure.

'Because I've heard it before—often,' he chuckled before he became serious. 'I didn't want it then and I don't want it now. Sheena's not my idea of a wife, she never was and in any case, I've a perfectly good wife already and I'm very well satisfied with her—I love her. I was a bad tempered fool and I lost her for a while but I've got her back now and I'll never let her go again.'

'You loved Sheena once,' she protested. 'You *must* have done—the deer fence, the Gairloch sands—I was only a kid at the time but I heard all about it . . .'

'I was also young and I was experimenting,' Piers was virtuous. 'How was I to know that a scruffy little schoolkid was going to grow up and wind herself around my heart—and as for Sheena, she was quite willing and I thought she understood there was nothing permanent involved. I made myself painfully clear, not only then but several times since . . .'

'You mean you've been . . .' Linnet scolded, pretending to outrage.

'No, I haven't and don't be so crude,' he growled back at her. 'My mother, for what she thought were the best of reasons thrust the young lady down my throat, encouraged her and I didn't want anybody to get the wrong ideas. By that time, you were growing up and a pair of blue eyes and a baby soft mouth were haunting me—getting between me and everything I did. Linnet, I know you're probably hungry and we ought to be getting back to the glen but I'm hungry as well—five years hungry. Would you refuse a starving man?'

'No,' she whispered it against his demanding mouth as she felt his arms tighten about her.

'Linnet,' he sighed it against her cheek. 'My darling, you've so much to forgive . . .'

'Hardly a thing,' her eyes were tender and the hand she raised to touch his face was gentle, her finger tips lingering on his unshaven chin. 'Darling, it wasn't your fault.'

'Yes it was,' he groaned. 'I'd wanted you so long,

scared stiff you'd meet someone your own age, someone who wasn't too old for you. I haunted that damned hotel just in case some smart alec made a pass at you. I didn't play fair with you, I didn't give you time to grow up properly but I didn't dare wait any longer although I knew you weren't ready,' he stifled her protest with a swift, hard kiss. 'I'd have taken the chance and made love to you only I was scared I'd frighten you off—you were so damn innocent about it all.'

'I loved you,' Linnet looked at him squarely. 'I'd have given you anything you asked. I'd always loved you. I tried not to but I couldn't help it. I couldn't even *see* another man, but I was a coward and when everything blew up in my face, I ran. Perhaps, if I'd been a bit older, known a bit more, I might not have run, but I couldn't bear for you to despise me, hate me. I could have faced anything but that,' she raised herself on one elbow and looked down at his face, 'Only you,' she whispered, 'there's never been anybody else, there never could be, not for me.'

'And I was rotten with jealousy,' he gathered her closely. 'That and my damned temper, I couldn't even think straight. I saw that painting and I think I went a bit mad . . .'

'It wasn't me,' she fingered the hard planes of his face tenderly. 'What I mean is, it *was* my face, Archie liked to paint that, he said it was Renaissance or something but that's all that was me about it—nothing else but I couldn't bear for you to be angry with me. It was as though I'd known all along that I wouldn't be allowed to be as happy as that—that dreams didn't come true so, I ran.'

'And I tried to find you,' he touched her tenderly. 'But it was as if you'd vanished from the face of the earth. I traced you as far as Inverary, but after that there was nothing and then, when you came back, all the old jealousy started again. I wanted you and I wanted to hurt you—I'd been hurting for so long and that damned bikini—it was doing things to me . . .'

'It was rather nice, wasn't it?' Her eyes twinkled while her fingers stroked and soothed.

'It was disgusting,' he snorted. 'You were lucky I didn't rape you on the spot.'

Linnet eased herself away from him and draped the blanket modestly about her nakedness. 'It might have been better if you had,' she teased. 'I think, if I'd been sure you could tell, I'd have encouraged you but somehow, I had the impression you didn't want to know,' and she dodged swiftly as he lunged for her.

'Minx,' his arms enveloped her, blanket and all and as he laid his cheek on the top of her head and his arms tightened, she knew it would take a long time and a lot of loving to make up for that five years.

'I'd even speculated on keeping you in the Room,' he admitted. 'I wanted to lock you away in a safe place where only I could get at you but I couldn't do it. You were afraid, you covered it up very well, but I could smell the fear on you and that night we spent together—it was sheer hell . . .'

'A drawn sword between us—well, it was at the beginning,' she chuckled softly. 'If anybody'd been listening, they'd have thought we were both mad. Piers,' she became serious, 'we're not mad now, are we?'

'I'm afraid so.' He smiled down at her upturned

face. 'Who else but a couple of loons would spend a night here when there was a perfectly good bed booked for us at the hotel.'

'A bed booked at the hotel?' she drew slightly away from him. 'Why?' Memory stirred and she wrinkled her forehead in a tiny frown. 'Piers, how did you know to come straight here and why were you ringing from Gairloch? What was all the panic about?'

'Coming straight here?' He slanted her a knowing smile. 'It was reasonable to suppose you'd look for shelter—you had to spend the night somewhere and this is the only place. Once I realised the direction you'd taken—and I could have beaten you for taking a chance like that—it was easy. I didn't think even you would attempt something as foolhardy as a walk like that when the weather was threatening. Did I frighten you that much?'

'No,' she was calm. 'But I wanted you to have a free choice, me or money . . .'

'A choice I made five years ago, mo creadh. No, it wasn't any choice at all, you were all that mattered to me. And when I thought of you last night, I was in a cold sweat. You could have fallen . . .'

'I did,' she confessed. 'I slipped on the scree, that's why I was in such a mess. I skidded all the way to the bottom and fell in the burn . . .'

'All to avoid a night with me?' His eyes glinted at her and she flushed at the tender mockery in them. 'I came round by the road to cut you off, saw the light here and made a beeline for it. I'd made up my mind we were going to have everything settled one way or the other. I didn't think I could stand another day of that arid thing we had going in the lodge.'

'And the phone calls, were you checking up on me?'

'In a way,' he admitted. 'You'd taken things much too quietly for my liking but that wasn't all. I wanted you safely out of the lodge and fixed up in the village until I was sure everything was safe. I'd already sent Matty and Old Jamie into Glenardh,' and at her puzzled look. 'Oh lord, I'd forgotten, you don't know anything about it, do you?'

'About what?'

'The mine,' Piers suddenly became curt and businesslike. 'Yesterday afternoon, a mine was spotted adrift in the Minch but the weather was closing in, there was a lot of haze about and they lost sight of it. Our boat picked up the message on the radio and they calculated that, allowing for the current, the drift and the tide, the thing ought to reach the coast somewhere near Lochardh. It must be as old as the hills and probably unstable, it could make a nasty mess of anything it bumped into—the wind and tide could even bring it right into the loch, that happened once before, about twenty years ago. That time, it grounded near the Otter so I thought the village would probably be the safest place. Darling, I don't want to, but we have to go; get dressed, will you?'

Linnet nodded serenely and as he went through the door, she glanced around the little, poor looking room. It had been heaven and she didn't want to leave it. Here, she'd found a greater happiness than she'd ever hoped for, it was the most beautiful place in the world but the world outside was knocking to get in. With a sigh, she reached into her bag for her clean jeans, shirt and underwear and scrambled herself into them,

topping them with her anorak against the chill of the
morning.

They were over halfway to Creevie before she
remembered and gave an embarrassed giggle. Piers
raised his eyebrows and turned his gaze away from the
road for a second to see what was amusing her. She
gave him a rueful grin.

'I forgot my wet things,' she explained. 'I left them
on the line over the fire. I was just thinking what
some lonely shepherd, all kirk and covenant, will think
one day when he walks into the croft and finds a pair
of jeans, a shirt and a couple of frillies hanging there!'

At the head of the glen, Piers stopped the Landrover to scan the loch anxiously. All trace of the
night's storm had gone, the sky was a pale, duck egg
blue under the morning sun and the loch was a shining
sheet of rippling water surrounded by the dark green
of the pines. Glenardh village seemed to be still asleep,
there was no commotion on the jetty and further
down, round the bend in the sheet of water, she could
pick out the lodge, huddled like a child's building
block under the trees, and against the sheen of the
water, the dark, forbidding bulk of Eilean Ardh stood
out plainly. She heard Piers' almost silent sigh of relief
and let her own breath out. Everything was all right,
nothing had happened to Piers' beloved glen and with
her relief came a little trickle of thought.

'The mine, Piers, it must have been what Ruby
meant when she said "danger with horns". I know I'm
being stupid but she's so often right.' She glanced at
him suspiciously. 'You surely didn't think—no, you
couldn't have—you've too much sense . . .'

'Last night, I wasn't in any mood to be sensible,' he

turned from his inspection of the loch and smiled at her ruefully. 'I was grudging every minute that kept me away from you—I didn't want to think about anything or anybody but you. I was praying so hard for a second chance, I couldn't think about anything else. Your Ruby's prediction never crossed my mind. I did things automatically while I planned what I'd say, what I'd do to convince you, to keep you. I even had a stray, noble idea I ought to give you more time. Good intentions!' he gave a snort of laughter. 'They didn't last long. I took one look at your white, frightened face—Linnet, I'll never frighten you again, I promise you that. We'll go home, we'll make a bonfire of that damned painting and I'll spend the rest of my life making up to you for every bit of grief, every bit of distress I've caused you ... We'll have a couple of days to ourselves—shut the world out and concentrate on each other then, when your Ruby arrives, we'll fix something up for her—a girl from the village if she needs company at the lodge—I shan't ever let you go.'

Linnet's hand stole into his as she leaned across, rested her head on his shoulder and closed her eyes in utter contentment. 'No, my darling,' she murmured softly. 'Don't ever let me go, not ever and please hurry, I want to get home.' She opened her eyes and looked down into the glen, along the strip of bright water and her eyes saw things differently. Eilean Ardh no longer looked grim and hostile—it looked strong, secure and somehow, welcoming.

Home is where the heart is and her heart had been here for so long, here with Piers. All she'd really done was to bring her numbed body back to join it—to be whole once more—to love and be loved. Would

Sheena be troublesome? She didn't think so and while she was pondering, her stomach gave a protesting rumble and Piers glanced at her quizzically.

'Breakfast first, little one. We'll probably have to get it ourselves, Matty will still be asleep somewhere in the village.'

'We'll cope,' she said sleepily and as she said it, she knew it was true. Together, they could cope with anything. Even Ruby!

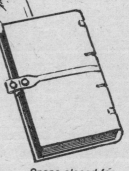